Pen to Print

Real People, Real Stories

This book has been produced with assistance from
The London Borough of Barking and Dagenham Library Service
Pen to Print: Real People, Real Stories Creative Writing Project 2016
with funding from The Arts Council, England Grants for the Arts.

LOTTERY FUNDED
Supported using public funding by
ARTS COUNCIL ENGLAND
London Borough of
Barking & Dagenham
lbbd.gov.uk

For Lisa, Daniel & Jack

Without you this would never have happened. You are my rock and rudder. You pick me up when I can't stand. Make me laugh when I don't want to and guide me to be the best person I can be.

Thank you xx

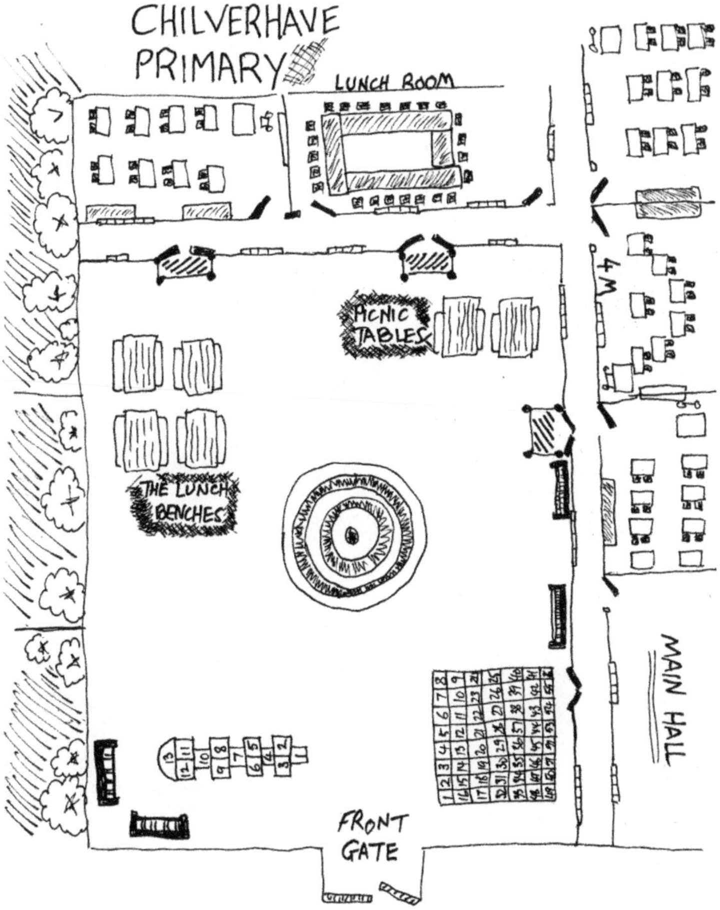
CHILVERHAVE PRIMARY
LUNCH ROOM
4W
PICNIC TABLES
THE LUNCH BENCHES
MAIN HALL
FRONT GATE

One

A Change from Boringist Things

Before we begin, it's probably a good idea to introduce the young man to our left. After all, he is the subject of the book. I think it's polite to do so.

His mum, Charlotte would no doubt agree. She always tells him, 'Charlie Robinson. How can people get to know you, if you never introduce yourself?'

He couldn't work out why she said that, because teachers knew him from the age of three and he never introduced himself. They always seemed to know who he was.

Anyway, as you've probably guessed, this is Charlie Robinson.

Charlie is nine years old and lives in what is apparently the most boringist house on the most boringist street in the most boringist town.

That's his pink house in the middle

of the street.

His mum says he shouldn't say boringist – because it's not a word, which would be fine and dandy, if she didn't make up words herself. Apparently she had the most 'lush' bowl of cereal this morning. Even though it looked like the most boringist bowl of horse food to Charlie.

He thinks he lives in the most boringist house in the most boringist street in the most boringist town because there never seems to be anything to do; except homework of course. There always seemed to be tons of homework.

Charlie lives in the middle of Chestnut Lane, one of two main streets in Chilverhave, which is a relatively large village or a small town; depending on your point of view.

It's called Chestnut Lane because many years ago, before he died, a beetroot and cattle farmer gave some of his land to the people that used to work for him. He didn't have any family and so, as a gesture, he created a village from the workers' houses on two sweeping farm tracks which ran around the farm like big half circles. They became Chestnut Lane and Acorn Drive. He lined Chestnut Lane with chestnut trees and Acorn Drive with oak trees.

The remainder of the village comprised his farm and a small market shop, which sold pretty much everything the village needed. This included fresh-baked bread, baked by the wives of the farm workers, eggs from the farm chickens, and milk from the farm cows and beetroot, of course. Everything else came into the village by van. It delivered groceries, cleaning products, toilet rolls, and newspapers. The man in the van also took post to the main post office in Brookehave, the town next to the village.

The village grew up around the farm. Over the years the number of houses on both streets doubled. There are now ten houses on each, which were built by the families of the families of the workers that originally worked on the Beetroot Cow farm. The tiny whip trees that lined the streets no longer flap and bend double in strong winds as they originally did. They now stand huge and straight opposite the rows of houses, deeply chiselled brown bark alluding to their history. Their thick arms are dressed in lush green for summer, signalling that they have earned their place in the world, and letting the wind know it holds no fear for them.

The farm isn't there anymore. It's now an outdoor centre where fitness types go to run, jump, climb, and get extremely muddy. They jump around and shout a lot. They aren't concerned about who was there before.

The memory of the farmer and his steaming Beetroot Cow farm faded over the years. But he gave the world Chilverhave and that's unlikely to fade.

Charlie's pink house was painted by one of the previous owners long before Charlotte bought it. She had intended to repaint it, but the colour grew on her each year. So, she left it. She bought the house after she and Charlie's dad, Paul, divorced, when he was five. They moved from Brentwood when she became a junior partner at a solicitor's firm. From the street, the house looks like any other. Two floors, windows and doors; no surprises, but it's a house with a secret. It's the only one in the street with a huge secret basement, hidden away from passing eyes.

They didn't use it for about a year – didn't even go down there. It was the place where all the extra bits and pieces were stashed during the move. Spare this, spare that; new things, old things and piles of tat.

It used to scare Charlie, until Mum turned it into her office.

His mind created a film in which the mad owner of the house buried the people he'd killed in the four hundred years he lived there. The reality was a little different when they got round to cleaning. The only bodies they found were spiders and woodlice – hardly scary stuff. He was cured from that moment on.

Above the basement is the ground floor, which consists of the dining room, living room, utility room and kitchen. To Charlie, a gorgeous posh pine forest of a kitchen. Beautiful cupboards constructed from the finest wood, hiding super expensive gadgets used to open bottles and cans with whizzing attachments for frothing. Drawers that closed themselves hiding highly polished knives, forks, and spoons. Long, honey-coloured slabs of pine concealing spinning carousel thingies and Mum's whizzy, slurpy, coffee gadgets.

The hallway from the front door extends to the back of the house and into the raised garden. But there's a sharp right turn about two metres from the front porch along the creaky worn oak floorboards. The hallway is decorated with simple elegance in light blue paint, smells of dried flowers and incense.

The stairs go up a flight of thirteen then open out right and left onto another hallway of creaky worn oak boards. Off the hallway are four bedrooms. To the left, the first door is Charlotte's room and bathroom, which Charlie believes is haunted, because he's never allowed in there.

The cornflower blue door matches the surrounding paintwork and has a driftwood plaque draped over the bulb handle with soft white rope. The plaque says:

As much as I love you

My dearest son

Keep your nose out Love, your Mum x

Next there's the small room, which belongs to Tiffany. She's from somewhere called O-pair, according to Charlie.

He assumed it was in Ireland, because she talks funny. Especially when shouting down the phone. She helps with the cooking, cleaning, and general stuff, and goes to university Tuesday and Thursday evenings. She is studying for an English degree that she hopes will help with her dream to be become an English teacher.

Opposite Tiffany's room is Charlie's, which is more definitely more 'lush' than his mum's horse food cereal. It's his man cave. The place he goes to when he needs to get away from the world and mull over the important issues that all nine-year-olds do.

Charlie's room stinks, according to his Mum. More often than not, his day-before socks and pants find their way under the bed or desk – to keep previous socks, bits of toast or pizza crust company. Charlie isn't the tidiest nine-year-old.

It's not a huge room. It's big enough for his bed, a wardrobe, a chest of drawers, a desk, a chair, a beanbag, and a few other things. And there's still enough room to roll around if the mood grabs him. His room is painted in a lovely shade of lilac white, which Mum chose and he said he would love. Even so, he adds to the ambiance whenever he can by covering every available space with superhero pictures and film posters.

Back along the hall, past the stairs, towards the window at the end, is the spare room. It was supposed to be a room for Charlie's brother or sister. But his mum and dad split because there was so much shouting.

This is the junk room. Among the piles of stuff there's an unused sewing machine and table. Charlotte went through a designer *'I'll make my own clothes'* phase and decided to buy the Yamaha X6400, which still sits in the corner without ever having been switched on. In the middle of the room is huge pile of clothes that people have donated and need to be sorted for the charity shop.

The mountain has been there for almost a week and is starting to infuse a certain fragrance that only old charity shop clothes can. She loves to collect for the charity shops in town, but has a real problem sorting the clothes.

Chilverhave has grown a little since the old days of the Beetroot Cow farm. It now has two small post offices, ten streets, one primary school, and a big school on the outskirts, close to Brookehave. But it doesn't have a big shop. It doesn't have Sainsbury's or any other large branded supermarket. If residents need anything other than the basics, they have to go into town at the weekend. In spite of this excitement, Charlie maintains that nothing ever happens in Chilverhave. Except one time, he recalls, when he was three.

A sudden explosion of noise had erupted as the neighbour, Mrs Watkins, ran into the street, shouting at the postman because he'd left his shoes under her bed. They must have been dirty or smelly. Charlie had no idea how he was going to deliver letters without his shoes.

So, that's the story of Charlie's boringist house in the boringist street in the boringist town. Or it would be, if he hadn't met Dudley in the middle of the school holiday last year.

Dudley became his best friend and a very good reason not to do French homework. *Je ne comprend pas* (I do not understand) became the standard phrase as he adopted his blank face, deserted Tiffany, and lots of boring '*ecouter et repeter*' (listen and repeat).

Charlie spent hours talking to him. He loved to listen to the incredible stories about the places he'd been to and the people he'd met. For example, Dudley had once met James Bond. Okay, that's not strictly true. He actually spent a summer underneath the sofa and sideboard at Daniel Craig's house.

But it's close enough.

It might be a good idea, at this point, to explain that Dudley is a spider.

To be more precise, he's a seven-legged spider. He lost the other one in an unfortunate rugby accident many years ago. Dudley loves playing rugby. He explained that he was in the scrum. The ref set the scrum and shouted 'CROUCH! ... BIND! ... SET!' They engaged and he came out with seven legs.

He did, however, have an artificial leg, which was made for him while he was at James Bond's house. The spiders living there have their own leg replacement division, overseen by a geeky spider known only as 'S'.

S designed Dudley a super bionic flipper of a leg – better than the original one. As a reminder of how he got it, he put one of his rugby boots on the foot.

And that was the day he became Dudley Clump. Because that's the noise he makes when he walks.

Two

The Duvet Tent and Jam Sandwiches

Stuck in the middle of the most boring summer holiday from school, Charlie was doing his best not to die from boredom. Chilverhave Primary clearly didn't want its pupils having fun. So the school provided mountains of homework to keep them busy. Charlie would gladly have got the dog to eat the pile of papers, if they had one. Unfortunately, he still had to work on Mum for that to happen.

Apparently it was important to understand that the angles inside a triangle add up to 180 degrees and that nine sixes are fifty-four. Charlie couldn't understand when he would ever use such information. People rarely approached him in the street and asked.

Bored, he tried to work out which picture was an unfolded cube, while teacher Tiffany flicked ferocious thumbs across her screen, clearly annoyed at someone. It was the only time she mumbled the words before dumping them on the screen. She must have been really annoyed today. She was planning a holiday to see her family in Ireland but it wasn't going well.

She didn't even notice Charlie slipping away to find something more interesting to do. He sort of gestured that he needed the toilet and she took her hand off the screen long enough to wave in the way people do when they've walked into a fart.

Charlie strolled along the hall towards the stairs. He stood at the bottom for a couple of seconds, listening intently. He was sure he could hear the spare room calling his name. He nodded to himself and donned the most serious face he could find. It was his duty as an explorer to investigate. Reaching for Tiffany's straw hat from the coat hooks, he stepped onto the stairway into the abyss. He wasn't sure if he would return. Anything could be hiding in that spare room.

He crouched and ninja fashion placed each foot on each stair, as though his life depended on the silence. He slithered upstairs and made it to the spare room without being spotted by evil forces. He grasped the handle, turned it, and opened the door slowly …

WHOOOOSHHHHHHH!

The game came to an abrupt end as two hundred years of old granny farts escaped into his face.

Mum had collected tons of stuff for charity shops *again*! The centre of the room was a heap of unsorted dusty clothes. Like a pile of old people to be sorted and sent out as nans and granddads to children that didn't have them.

Charlie spotted what looked like an old case in the corner of the mass. Half in, half out, dragged down into the quicksand by coat arms and trouser legs. He approached carefully, back in explorer mode. He grabbed the handle of the case and started to pull. Grrrrr! Arghhhh! Pffffttt! After a couple of minutes wrestling he was puffed.

It would not budge!

He surveyed the item, looking for somewhere to wedge a hand or foot. Unable to find any leverage, he decided to leave the casualty to die in the quicksand. As he turned to go something caught his eye. There were stickers on the case! He imagined it had travelled to interesting places like Egypt, Australia, Greece, and America. Maybe it contained ancient scary things from Egypt. Pyramids, pharaohs and mummies had been covered in homework with Tiffany.

Curiosity got the better of him. He decided to attack the pile of arms and legs with renewed vigour. Tipping his hat, he rolled up the sleeves of his tee shirt and got stuck in, following arms of shirts and sweaters and arriving at legs of trousers. A few minutes of manic grabbing and throwing ensued. Brown and grey flew this way and that as a swirl of old, musty, sweaty people filled the room. A breathless Charlie stopped for a second, got his bearings, and realised he was buried under the pile. His gaze fell to the floor and he caught his breath. The prize was right in front of him. A small, battered, brown and beige case, with shiny metal corners, about the size of a sofa cushion, covered with stickers – 'Welcome to Los Angeles', 'Greetings from Tokyo', 'Savoy Hotel Rome', 'Welcome to the Hotel Du Mont Paris'.

But the most important was the address sticker, which read: 'If found please return to Daniel Craig, No7 Doris Rust Drive, Collington, Hampshire RG24.'

Charlie couldn't believe his luck. Actor Daniel Craig's case! The suitcase he might have taken around the world while filming the James Bond movies. Charlie gingerly turned the small key in the old, slightly rusty lock … Clunk! The lock dropped into place. He placed his thumb on the square next to the keyhole and pushed the button to the side. 'Splachungggg!' The latch sprang open and slapped the back plate.

His heart jumped in his chest.

A tug cracked the dusty seal and he leaned in as the top half of the case lifted slowly. As his eyes widened to see the dark interior, a million thoughts rushed through his head.

Maybe there was spy stuff left in the case? Perhaps there was a magnetic watch or exploding pen? Or a satellite tracking device? Maybe a miniature camera? Maybe James Bond was watching as he opened the case. Perhaps it was part of a plan to defeat evil forces and he needed Charlie's help?

The lid groaned on rusty hinges as it opened and light revealed the interior. Charlie rose up on his knees to get a better look. It looked empty. Then something moved in the corner and he froze. A black shape turned, unfolded, and popped up in front of him. He tried to move but couldn't. Welded to the spot he just closed his eyes and hoped for the best. Nothing happened.

A minute or more of nothingness passed and he slowly opened his eyes – left at first and then the right. It took a second to adjust to the shadowy day lit room and then he noticed another nose in front of his, above which rested large black plastic glasses over blue eyes, and underneath the nose was a massive set of bright white teeth.

Keeping his head still, Charlie quickly scanned left and right and noticed legs, legs, and more legs. The white teeth curved into a smile. He was nose to nose with … the biggest spider ever!

'Arrrrrrrrrrrrrrrrrrrrrgggggghhhhhhhhhhhh!'

He jumped up and bolted out of the spare room. His scream followed him down the hall and into his room. Before he even knew what was happening, he was sitting cross legged under the duvet with his head torch on. Safe!

The duvet tent was his refuge from the dark and the monsters that crept around while the family slept. Monsters that overfilled the bins, hid the TV remote, and put washing up in the sink, according to Charlie's mum.

Heart beating like an insane drummer he reached under his bed for the blackcurrant drink left there the day before. He quickly pulled his arm back into safety and guzzled from the sports cap.

‘Any chance of a drink?’ said a very distinguished bass voice from behind him.

Charlie’s stomach turned as his body did.

‘I do apologise, Sir. I seemed to have scared you. Don’t be alarmed.’ The spider beamed a huge smile and held out a leg, as if to shake hands. ‘Allow me to introduce myself. The name’s Clump. Dudley Clump.’

Mortified, Charlie found himself automatically raising his own hand to shake the approaching leg. The spider gripped his hand firmly and shook twice. He tilted his head towards Charlie, raised his eyes in an expectant fashion and said; ‘And you are?’

Staring in disbelief he stuttered, ‘I’m … er … I’m … er … Charlie Robinson.’

Dudley Clump nodded.

‘Pleased to meet you Charlie Robinson. I’m sorry I scared you. It wasn’t my intention – and could I have some of your drink? I was in that case for days and I’m parched.’

Charlie blankly handed over his drink. Dudley Clump took a massive glug, wiped his mouth and handed the bottle back.

‘Thank you so much Sir. Or may I call you Charlie? It was so dry in that case. I have no idea how I ended up there. One minute I was asleep in the corner of the case, then I got shut in, rattled about, and bashed. I thank you so much for letting me out. You have no idea how stuffy it can get in a closed suitcase. And I’m not awfully fond of the dark. By the way … where am I?’

Charlie, now slightly calmer, looked at the spider in disbelief. ‘You can talk?’

‘Of course,’ said Dudley Clump. ‘All spiders can talk. Most humans just can’t hear us.’

‘Then how come I can hear you? Am I dreaming or something?’ Charlie enquired.

Dudley looked quizzical. He took a moment, contorting his face into thinking shapes, then brought a front leg to his face, cupped his chin as though deep in thought, looked up, and shrugged all eight shoulders.

‘No idea Sir. But I’m glad you can.’

It seemed to break the ice.

That afternoon the pair spent hours talking under the duvet tent, only pausing to get supplies from the kitchen. Charlie made a feast from a pile of badly made strawberry jam sandwiches, a family packet of Cheesy Puffs, and a huge bottle of cherryade.

They were set for the evening.

CHEESY
PUFFS

Three

The Scrum, Secret Spiders, and the Artificial Leg

That first night in the duvet tent, Charlie noticed something different about Dudley– as if being a talking spider wasn't enough. It was a shiny silvery metal something which had a white plastic sleeve about halfway down, painted with a bright red George Cross.

Curiosity got the better of him.

'Dudley, I hope you don't think I'm being rude, but where did you get your artificial leg from?'

Dudley broke off from his sandwich. Jam and crumbs stuck to his fuzzy face. Words found their way out between chews.

'It's not rude at all, Sir. I lost my leg playing rugby.' He went back in for another bite.

Confusion etched on Charlie's face. "Don't be silly, Spiders don't play rugby."

"Oh yes, they do," Dudley replied firmly, swinging around. A string of jam dangled from his spider beard. "I've played rugby for years. I even played in the Six Nations for England. That's where I had to be stretchered off, having lost the bottom half of my front leg in a scrum." No sooner had the last word left his lips than he was buried back in the pile of sandwich.

Stunned into silence, Charlie sat for a few minutes before the next question formed in his head.

"Hang on a minute. Spiders playing rugby for England and losing legs in a scrum? I must be dreaming. I need to wake up."

Dudley turned again, jammy lipstick all over his face. 'Okay, I'll explain. I've played rugby since I was a spiderling. I grew up playing rugby. We had a team at the house where I was born.'

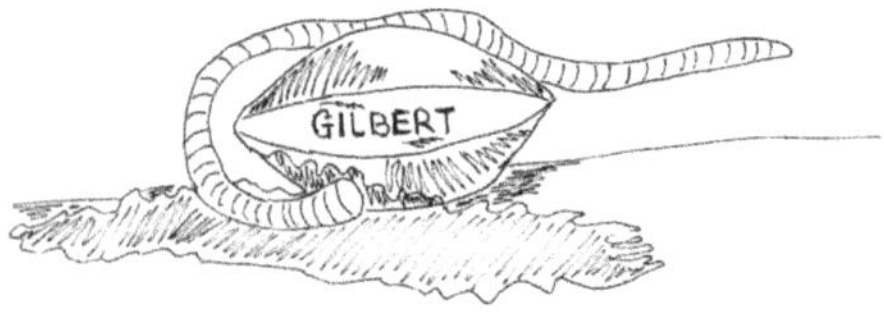

He explained that his team, the Sofa Cardinals, had played in a league with other teams who lived at the house. There were teams of spiders, woodlice, beetles, centipedes, and worms.

The worms were rubbish at rugby, due to their lack of arms. But they insisted on forming a team, because there were more of them than any of the other mini beasts and they said it was wrong to leave them out. More often than not they brought an abrupt end to a game by jumping on the ball and covering it with a mass of snotty slime.

The centipedes won more matches than anyone else. They thought they were better than all the other teams. But they only won because they had more arms. In the last match before Dudley left the house, his team beat the Spare Room Sharks in the Sideboard Sevens tournament – a title they hadn't won since before he was born.

The Spare Room Sharks were a team of centipedes with a mad South African Dung Beetle head coach. They were often seen running up and down the garden in groups, shouting loudly: 'READY! ... SET! ... SQUEEZE!' They were the team to beat. Which made the 35–5 victory even sweeter than usual.

The spider got his first England cap after scoring two tries in the centipede victory.

In February each year, teams of spiders, woodlice, earwigs, and beetles from the six European rugby nations gathered at a house in Twickenham to play the Six Nations championship. In their first match, England were 15–5 up against a team of French wood beetles when the referee called for a scrum close to the wood beetles goal line.

Sensing a scoring opportunity, Dudley and the other forwards huddled together and mumbled tactical rugby things, then squashed together, ready for the ball to be rolled in.

HEEEEEAAAAVVE!! Came the collective shout, as the England spiders pushed the beetles back and the ball came out. Dudley pulled his head out, ready to chase the crowd, but promptly fell down as he tried to run. He looked down and, to his horror, the bottom half of his front leg was missing. In true rugby tradition he jumped up and tried to run it off. But when he saw the other part of his leg on the ground he fainted and collapsed in a heap.

Medics rushed Dudley to the makeshift medical room in an old shoe at the bottom of the wardrobe in a bedroom. Unfortunately, the shoes were destined for the charity shop that day, with Dudley in them. When the medics returned the wardrobe was empty. Everything had been whisked away.

That was how he ended up at Daniel Craig's house.

Mr Craig's housekeeper bought the shoes from the charity shop to wear for work because they looked comfortable.

On arrival, Dudley was discovered by the house spiders that lived under the sofa. They extracted him from the shoe and took him to the Top Secret facility behind the fridge in the kitchen. He looked up from his stretcher as they descended upon him like a team of well- drilled circus performers dressed in white coats. They glided in without a sound, directing each other with nods and nudges.

'Ahh, ayy, hupp, ho!' they eventually said, and Dudley was hoisted on shoulders and swept away.

Seconds later, they had made it down the hallway, into the kitchen, and around the back of the cooker. The group were greeted by a large silver door which had a number pad to the right.

The lead technician was easily identifiable because he had the words LEAD TECHNICIAN on the back of his white coat. He approached the number pad, reached out a long geeky leg and tapped in the PIN to open the door. A short pause was followed by a series of slow metallic clunks and a hiss, then the big silver door swung open to reveal a bright light. They walked through it, then everything went dark.

Dudley woke to a soft Scottish voice. 'Hello. Are you still with us, dearie?' He opened his eyes to a white hat on top of dark brown hair, leaning over him with a cup of tea and two shortcake biscuits.

'Where am I? What happened?' he said. 'The last thing I remember I was playing rugby.' As his eyes adjusted to the bright light, he noticed more of the crisp white room. He seemed to be in hospital.

'I dunna noo aboot that dearie. I juss work in recovery. It's oor job ta get ya back on yer feet. Would ya like a biscuit with ya tea?'

The door squeaked and opened and a rather round spider wearing a white coat glided into the room. He walked to the end of the bed and picked up Dudley's chart. Then he nodded and blurted out a torrent of words without taking a single breath.

'Good morning, Sir. If I can call you Sir. Only we didn't have a name for your chart. We looked in your clothes, but they didn't offer any clues. By the way, why would a spider be wearing rugby kit? Anyway, how is the new leg?'

He finished as quickly as he had started.

'WHHHHHHHAAAAAAAAAAAAAT?' shouted a shocked Dudley. The bed sheets flew up like a parachute and his gaze fixed on a titanium artificial half leg with a foot at the end. The sheet cascaded and landed on him, making him look like a ghost. He slowly pulled the sheet down and stared at the doctor, who smiled an innocent smile.

Very deliberately Dudley said, 'Do you mind telling me what on earth is going on? One minute I'm playing rugby. The next I'm in some kind of secret facility and I have a new leg.'

'Well,' said the doctor. 'S thought you might like a new leg.' He explained that S was the head of the facility and was involved in some very 'hush, hush' science stuff for the government. Apparently some of the research involved the development of titanium artificial limbs for athletes competing in the Paralympics. So he decided to test their new model by letting Dudley have one.

And that's how Dudley Clump became the only spider in history to have an artificial leg.

Four

Men Pack their Own Lunch

The last two weeks of the school holiday flew by for Charlie. There never seemed to be enough time to listen to the endless adventures of his new best friend. Nothing else held his interest; every moment away from Dudley was an irritation. Conversations with Mum were reduced to 'Yes, Mum. Yes, Mum! … YES, MUM! Can I go now?' Food was wolfed down or prodded in an attempt to fake interest. It was much more interesting to spend his time with Dudley and a packet of Cheesy Puffs.

Their bromance blossomed.

Then the holiday was over. The day finally arrived for Charlie to return to school, and year five at Chilverhave Primary beckoned. Charlie woke at 6.30 a.m. to Mum's school alarm voice.

'Charlie Robinson! I'm not going to call you again. You're going to be late if you don't get your carcase moving. Please don't make me come up there.'

Throwing back the duvet, caged cheesy farts were let loose into the bedroom. Yawning and stretching he decided he would tell Mum he wasn't going to school any more. He would be a solicitor like her. She seemed to do okay. He warbled uncertain protest from the bathroom.

'Mum? Do I have to go back to school? School's rubbish. Can't I leave school and be a solicitor like you?'

'Get readyyyy!' she said seriously. The words raced upstairs to box his ears.

'Okay, okay.' He knew her serious voice.

The next step was growly. Nobody needed growly Mum. Wild animals on those wildlife programmes where lions chase and eat wildebeest didn't need growly Mum. She could easily scare lions away from their dinner. Growly Mum could make angry charging hippos stop and apologise for the inconvenience. Even crocodiles would give up the chance of an easy meal and swim away to avoid growly Mum.

So, to avoid a growly Mum episode, in whirl of arms and legs, he leapt out of his smelly pyjamas and into fresh school clothes. Before leaving the room he grabbed the duvet corner and flung it over the crinkled sheets and pillow dent. A rugby boot on shiny metal emerged from under the bed.

Charlie had made Dudley a home from home under the bed from a school shoe box. He borrowed a yellow car cleaning sponge from the cleaning box under the kitchen sink and a new polishing cloth from the cabinet in the bathroom. They fitted the shoe box perfectly. Dudley had a bed and a home. In an attempt to make his friend as comfortable as possible, Charlie even rigged up his old head torch in the springs under the bed.

Having never had a spider friend before, he had no idea if they did spidery things in the middle of the night. If they did he was pretty sure they had super night vision. He'd read it somewhere. But, just in case, Dudley had a night light.

'Morning Dudley, can't stop.' He hurried, gathering school essentials. 'Good morning, Sir. What's all the commotion?'

'I'm back to school today. I hate the first day back. Stupid school! Must rush or Mum will turn growly. You don't want to be around when she does that.'

'Can I come with you? I've never seen a school.'

Dudley tilted his fuzzy head down, raised his eyebrows, and looked over the top of his glasses in anticipation.

Charlie smiled and nodded enthusiastically. But there was a problem. He'd never taken a spider to school. Where would Dudley hide?

Pockets? Not big enough and people might ask questions about fuzzy legs sticking out. Coat? No. Book bag? No. Nobody needs a teacher having a heart attack from an unexpected pop-up.

LUNCHBOX! Yes!

He grabbed it from the top of the wardrobe and placed it on the bed. He gripped the rolled sleeve of his sweater and wiped the dust from the shiny red American-style trunk, then nodded to Dudley, who saluted and jumped in. One last whirlwind of school preparation and Charlie was ready. He bounced downstairs with his lunchbox and into the kitchen.

'Ready, Mum,' he announced with a smile, placing the lunchbox on the counter. Mum was on the phone.

'I asked Ola to copy those documents and send them out by messenger urgently. Just a moment … Charlie, I've made you chicken salad sandwiches. I'll put them in your lunchbox—' She was being multitasking Mum, floating around the kitchen like an octopus, phone held to her ear with her shoulder while making sandwiches, washing dishes, and cleaning the floor. The sandwich holding tentacle reached out and started to open the lunchbox.

NOOOOOOooo!

'NOOOOOO!' he shouted, running towards the counter with outstretched arms. It cut through everything like an alarm. Mum's tentacles ceased their flurry of activity, falling to her side. Slowly placing the sandwich on the counter next to the lunchbox she burned a hole in Charlie with a disapproving gaze.

'I'll call you back.' She leaned across the counter and very deliberately placed the phone back where it lived.

'Excuse me, Sir. What was that?'

Oh no. Growly Mum! His thoughts became a panicked mass in his head, then a clearing appeared. 'Errrr, well.' It took a few seconds but … got it! He said, 'I'm not a baby any more, Mum, and a man should put his own lunch in his own lunchbox.'

The comment stopped her in her tracks. She paused for a minute then replied, 'Well, okay Mr Man. I apologise. In

future I will leave your lunch on the counter and you can pack it yourself. By the way, do men still eat crisps and jelly snakes?'

Charlie looked at his shoes 'Err … yes, please,' he mumbled, having been taken down a peg. 'Thanks, Mum.' He beamed a knowing smile, placed his lunch in the box next to Dudley, and they were off.

Five

Phyllis Merrick, Flying Pens, and Rumours

Charlie arrived at school. He kissed Mum goodbye and joined the line of kids going in through the main entrance, which was an old iron gate about two metres wide, divided in two and attached to weather-pitted brick pillars on either side. Not wide enough to get a car through. Flaky old black gargoyles sat on top, looking down intently, and telling each other stories about every pupil that ever walked through.

The steady line of arrivals became a herd that worked its way across the playground towards the open doors, through and into the main hall.

The same thing happened after every summer holiday. Like an odd recycling centre for children, endless streams of cars approached the school, slowing only to toss out badly dressed children.

The main hall was where you found out if you'd won the lottery with a good teacher or one of those dusty old relics that could barely hear and should have retired to the store cupboard years ago. The kind of waxwork you'd expect to see stuffed and being used as a bookshelf in book corner.

Charlie's class didn't win the lottery and that meant year five would be interesting. As his class (5M) was announced, he realised they'd got Miss Merrick – Miss Phyllis Merrick.

At sixty-four, Phyllis had been a teacher for a gazillion years. The head teacher wanted her to retire, but couldn't ask as the school might fall down if she left, in much the same way as the Tower of London would collapse if the ravens flew away.

As a short, round woman with spindly legs, fat arms, and a big head, Miss Merrick must have found clothes shopping difficult. She almost looked like an egg on chopsticks. On top of her head sat long, straight, silver hair, pulled back and rolled into a croissant and speared with a sparkling hair slide.

The kids at school were convinced pale Phyllis was a vampire. They talked about her in small groups as she glided around the school, whispering busily as she passed. She didn't help their assumptions by wearing the longest skirts possible on her short body. And, although she pulled the waistband up under her chest, the skirt still hid her shoes, swishing the floor in a way that suggested she was floating along, followed by a dusty waft from the 1970s.

Despite the danger of getting bitten on the neck and having your blood sucked out, it was easy to learn in her lessons. Unlike modern teachers, she actually made learning interesting and fun. Part of that fun was avoiding flying objects because Phyllis had random physical tics caused by Tourette's syndrome.

A day in Miss Merrick's class was an adventure. More often than not, while marking the register, she would have a monumental left arm twitch and her pen would fly off towards the classroom door. Anyone entering would have to duck, or risk being impaled by a flying biro.

Any other teacher might be embarrassed, but Phyllis was so used to the tics that she didn't break stride when marking the register. She kept a tub of fifty black biros on her desk and used almost all of them during the day.

'Daniel Peterson?' 'Here, Miss!' 'Nathan Cartwright?' 'Here, Miss!'

FLICK! … WHIZZ! … BANG!

'Molly Perkins?'

As pen monitor, Molly had to collect flung pens from around the classroom at break and lunchtime and put them back in the box ready to be flung the following day. Her reward was extra sweets from the sweet jar that Miss Merrick kept by her desk as an incentive for students to do their best work.

Charlie sat next to Robert, his best friend from year four. They were happy to be reacquainted and shared stories of their adventures over the summer. Charlie couldn't say anything about Dudley because everyone would think he was mad. But a voice in his head wanted to

tell the world. It kept telling Charlie it would be okay to let the odd detail slip, but he kept telling the voice to shut up.

Robert's enormously long stork legs made him the tallest at the school. He towered over the year sixes, who were almost two years older, and he was almost as tall as the male teachers. He never measured himself, but his friends guessed he was about nine feet. He took after his mum, who used to be a professional netball player. A flamingo of a woman, she strode around on legs like the jugglers and clowns at carnivals. She ran her own sports coaching company and always wore tracksuit trousers and a tee shirt emblazoned with her company design. Robert said that old ladies and short people asked her to get things on high shelves at the supermarket, which she did willingly because it made her feel powerful.

The friends sat at the first desk in front and to the right of Phyllis. White-painted brick walls ran around the classroom, broken up by large red and blue felt noticeboards, ready to accept the year's artistic efforts. The last of the strong autumn sunlight bounced around the room, occasionally blinding them.

The school hadn't changed the old scratched and gouged honey-coloured desks from previous years. They told tales of past pupils who had scratched their names in badly spelled statements. Charlie wondered if 'STEVE' who 'WOZ ERE '86' now realised that WOZ was not how 'was' was spelled.

The remaining flaky scratched desks were arranged in a golden horseshoe so Phyllis could see everyone. To the right of Charlie and Robert were Nathan and Bethany, two other members of the friends group from the previous year.

Nathan had a super power. He seemed to absorb

information through his toes. It didn't matter what the subject, Nathan always found a way to be the smartest. The group was sure he was going to be a game designer or would find a way to rule the world. He was that clever. But he complained, mostly about being ill. Nathan said he had a curved spine and one leg shorter than the other, which made him walk with a limp. When someone pointed out he walked normally he suddenly developed an exaggerated stiff leg, which he threw out in front of his good one. He apparently also had one arm longer than the other and his toenails grew to the left. Nobody believed a word of it. But he was fun to be around, so the group just brushed off his complaining, laughed when he was caught out, and carried on.

Bethany was probably the most 'normal' person in the group. Normal height, normal hair, normal features. Just normal. The only thing that made Bethany stand out from the crowd was her laugh snort. When Bethany laughed everyone knew it. She sounded like an English attack goose chasing off swans and demanding bread at the park.

Then there was Charlie, who was still small enough to duck under the dining room table when playing on it with Mum. Ginger hair, eyebrows, and freckles that seemed to breed in the sun. Charlie, who had a talking spider in his lunchbox.

Nothing much happened that first day. As usual, there were announcements about the term ahead. There were handouts from teachers that made great bedding for backpack monsters, folders handed out for all the homework that would pile up, subject books and summaries galore. The most momentous thing that day was the announcement that a new student would be joining the class – a boy named Billy Clarke.

No sooner had Miss Merrick made the announcement than the rumours started.

Billy Clarke was known by everyone in class as Clarkie. Clarkie, a problem student and a horrible bully of a child, expelled from his previous school for hitting a teacher. No other school would take him. His parents had to beg Chilverhave Primary and promise there wouldn't be a repeat of his behaviour. It was the only school in the area to offer him a place. He would arrive at the end of September.

What followed was the longest three weeks Charlie and his classmates had ever endured. An impending doom threatening to change everything they had known since nursery. Everyone knew Clarkie was a horrible person. The question was, would he be a bully at Chilverhave Primary?

Or had he changed?

Six

The Monster and Clarkie's Arrival

Billy Clarke's anticipated arrival put everyone in limbo. The kind of limbo you can't escape. Like waiting for a dentist's appointment, just knowing you'll have an injection.

Like fish, small groups gathered in corners of the playground, chattering about what Clarkie would and wouldn't do, wriggling in tight fives and sixes, until someone left with a rumour and a worry for a new group somewhere else in the playground.

Clarkie did the worst of worst things anyone could do in the school world. He had hit a teacher. He may as well be a murderer. It was okay to imagine the horrendous things you could to teachers. In the same way it was okay to imagine force-feeding parents stewed cabbage or hanging them from the ceiling by their toenails. But that was letting off steam. Nobody ever hit a teacher. Clarkie must have been a complete nutcase.

Everyone knew of Clarkie, but nobody knew what he looked like. He was a myth. A horror story that everyone knew and hoped wasn't real.

Each member of the group had a vision of Clarkie but didn't dare say anything. Letting anyone in the playground know you had any real feelings about anything was a serious no-no. The playground mafia were ruthless. It was okay to chatter about rubbish. Girls were allowed to be girly and a little dramatic. But boys had to be hard as nails. Nothing bothered boys. Chocolate bars up in price, no problem. Spam fritters for school dinner, easy peasy. Zombie apocalypse, pah! No big deal. Scared about Clarkie coming to the school – now that was lame!

It was those throwaway single word nicknames that cut the deepest. They were important for boys and girls to avoid. Nobody wanted to go through three years with the nickname Chicken Charlie or FleaBag Robinson. Getting good grades was difficult enough, without the added pressure of a horrible nickname.

So, boys, or blokes, were hard.

Charlie's mind produced a caricature bully of enormous proportions: eight feet tall, with shoulders and chest wide enough to block out the sun; massive, bulging, concrete arms ending with hammer fists. It was a picture that left no doubt – it screamed 'bully'.

Over time Charlie's vision of Clarkie wreaked havoc in his dreams. One particularly difficult night, he chased and trapped a group of children in the classroom. Charlie cowered in the corner as the bully bore down on him. On the far side of the classroom Miss Merrick was in mid-air, pinned to the noticeboard with dozens of biros.

It was not good!

Even talking with Dudley didn't ease the increasing tension. The more stressed Charlie got, the more their conversations were limited to 'hi' and 'bye'. Gradually Charlie was descending into a nightmare.

September days flew off the calendar like birds freed from a cage. Then it happened, at Friday afternoon registration. Miss Merrick announced that Billy Clarke would be in class on Monday. Charlie's heart sank and his stomach gurgled in the way it did when he was really hungry. Oh GOD! he thought.

Somebody pressed the fast forward button for the weekend. Hours seemed like minutes in the countdown to

Monday. The more Charlie tried to hang on to time, the faster it slipped through his fingers. Before he knew it, 'Charlie Robinson!' Mum called. 'DO NOT make me come up there.'

Charlie blinked his crusty eyes under the duvet. The dreaded Monday had arrived. He grabbed either side of his pillow, buried his head, and shouted. 'No, No! NO, NO! NOOOOOOOOOOO!'

A throat clearing 'Uh-hum' came from beside him under the duvet. He emerged from the pillow, nose to nose with a stern looking Dudley.

'I haven't said much over the last couple of weeks. I thought you would tell your BEST FRIEND what was going on in your head when you were ready. But you didn't. So I'm asking. WHAT … IS … WRONG?'

Charlie couldn't contain it any more. He couldn't be brave any more. He opened his mouth and everything came out. The fear of Clarkie, the nightmares and anger at himself for not being hard like the other boys at school.

'Ahhhhhhhhh. Now I get it,' Dudley exclaimed. 'So you've been worried and putting pressure on yourself. You know, things aren't usually as bad as you think they'll be. I'm sure young Mr Clarke just found himself in a difficult situation. I doubt he's a monster.'

Soothed by the words of his friend, Charlie calmed a little. He gathered his thoughts, his lunch, and his friend, and made his way to the car.

As they approached the school, the feeling returned in the pit of his stomach. He gripped the lunchbox so tight the lid popped open slightly. Dudley gave him a serious look and fist pump. *You can do this*! he mouthed. It did the trick. Charlie snapped back to reality, composed himself, and went into school.

'Daniel Peterson?'

'Here, Miss!'

'Nathan Cartwright?'

'Here, Miss!'

FLICK! … BANG!

'Molly Perkins!'

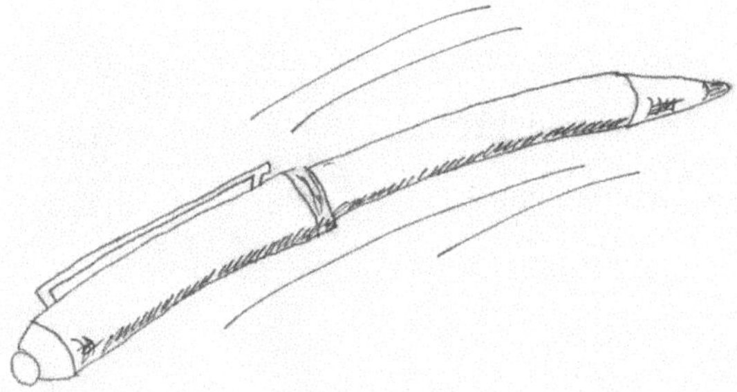

Miss Merrick welcomed the new week with her usual assortment of flying biros. She finished taking the register and stood up.

'Morning, 5M. Today we have a new pupil joining the class.' She gestured to someone sitting at a desk in front of her. 'Class, can you please welcome our new arrival, Billy Clarke.' A small, well-dressed child with neatly styled blond hair stood in front of the class.

Miss Merrick liked her class to repeat things back to her. They parroted in unison.

'GOO-D MOR-NING BILL-Y CLAR-KE!'

Charlie was astonished. He looked normal. Not at all like the monster in his head. He wasn't eight feet tall. He didn't have a chest and shoulders wide enough to block out the sun. Or arms and fists with more bulges than a bag of cats.

Then confusion set in. *How could this little thing beat up a teacher*? he wondered. Calm washed over him. He opened his lunchbox and gave Dudley a quick thumbs up. Things were okay. His worries were over.

Or so he thought …

Seven

The Lunchbox and the Ginger Midget

The playground couldn't get enough of Billy Clarke. He strutted around like a pop star with an entourage and loved it. The short designer-blond smug smile on legs swaggered from bench to lunch tables, stopping momentarily to sit. When he did, crowds gathered and arms thrust things at him.

'Want some of my crisps, Billy?'

'Billy, do you need a drink?'

'Want a sweet?'

Billy, Billy! BILLLLY!

Mr Clarke absorbed his new found infamy with gusto. Boys either wanted to be his friend or stayed out of his way. Girls were either attracted to his confidence or disgusted by his attitude. Either way, he was the talk of the town for a while.

Things change quickly at primary school. By the end of that first week the initial fascination with Mr Clarke was dying down and playground life was getting back to normal.

Some girls had gone back to juggling balls, sending sneaky texts, and playing games on their mobile phones.

Others were skipping and jumping around on the hopscotch lines painted by the front gates. The geeky types had gone back to reading at the picnic tables, debating who would eventually be doctors and lawyers and who would be working at the local chicken shop. Everyone else had gone back to what they were doing before Mr Clarke's arrival.

As expected, Billy Clarke attracted the kind of people who didn't have friends because they were either nasty or loners. He was a famous person to them, because he had hit a teacher at his previous school. Kids didn't hit teachers, so he was something special – someone who would do what nobody else was prepared to.

As the weeks went by, a new group emerged in playground world, as the new master made his presence felt. The first incident happened on Monday after the October half-term holiday.

Mr Clarke and his group decided to sit at the picnic tables where the geeky kids usually sat to eat their packed lunches. Billy was sitting on a table while his henchmen spread themselves between the benches, next to those already eating. Billy caught their eyes and raised his eyebrows.

'Got any crisps?' he enquired in a slow, sinister tone.

'No. Only cheese biscuits,' replied one, showing the packet.

'They'll do.' Billy leaned forward and swiped the packet before the sentence had left his lips.

Molly Perkins had just finished collecting Miss Merrick's flying biros from morning registration and joined her friends at the picnic tables. She walked around the worn brown picnic table to find her usual spot. Mr Clarke slid down from the table and was now sitting next to a henchman on one of the side benches.

There was just enough space for Molly. She sat in her spot but felt uncomfortable that things were different and there seemed to be an air of tension. But she unpacked her ham and tomato sandwiches, crisps, and drink anyway.

She arranged everything on the table as she always did, then closed her bag and slid it under the bench. She extracted the sandwiches from their wrapping and placed them on the napkin her mum always put in the box for her. Then she unscrewed the cap of her drink, which hissed its lemonade reply.

Mr Clarke seemed to take all the available space – clearly in an attempt to cause friction, the way bullies usually do. They push and push until they get the reaction they want. Then the war of words or fists comes. If the reaction doesn't come they win anyway because they make people afraid of them.

Molly politely asked if he could move up.

'No,' he sniped. 'If you don't like it, go and sit somewhere else.' He shuffled closer and bumped Molly along the bench with his backside.

'HELLLP … arrrrrrrgh!' CRUNCH! Molly didn't realise she was so close to the end of the bench. Landing on the tarmac she grazed her arm and elbow. As she fell her drink wobbled and tipped, soaking her as she lay beside the table, crying.

Mr Clarke led the chorus of cruel laughter and pointing as a wet Molly curled up, surrounded by crisps and pieces of sandwich. Everyone else froze in stunned silence. Mrs Lowther heard the commotion and rushed to help.

'My God, Molly, what happened?' She picked Molly up and examined her bloody arm. 'We need to get you to the medical room,' she said urgently, collecting Molly's belongings.

As they walked past, Molly stared at Mr Clarke, who gazed back with a pointed sneer as though to warn her. It worked. When questioned about the incident she said she had misjudged the end of the bench and fell.

Mr Clarke had settled in and was making his mark, as Charlie discovered later that week.

Thursday. As usual, Dudley hitched a ride in Charlie's lunchbox. They sat at the picnic tables before everyone else came out, sharing a packet of Cheesy Puffs while working out what they would do if a zombie outbreak ever really happened.

Mr Clarke and his flock of henchmen noticed Charlie. A series a nudges and whispers and they changed direction at the same time. Like a flock of very annoying birds they descended upon Charlie.

Mr Clarke saw Charlie close his lunchbox quickly. The flock quickly gathered around.

'Oooooooo. What's in the box, Chaz? Let's have a look?' Charlie looked around at the dark wall of henchmen standing over him. He stopped at Clarkie's ice-blue glare and immaculately gelled blond hair. The look suggested he was a spoilt child. The latest Ysas watch in purple and Desmond Falk designer shoes said the rest.

‘It’s just lunch,’ Charlie replied. He was cold with fear and felt sick. The shivers started.

‘Prove it!’ Clarkie raised his voice.

Trying to make them think he wasn’t scared, Charlie decided to take control of the situation and make a joke. He had to protect Dudley at any cost.

‘Prove what? That I’ve got chicken salad sandwiches? You want me to open this box and ask my sandwiches to identify themselves?’ Here Charlie adopted a deep, military voice. ‘You? Sandwich. Where are your papers? Identify yourself. Are you chicken or ham?’

Clarkie’s henchmen collapsed into laughter. Clearly angry, Clarkie edged closer and lunged forward. Instinctively, like a mantis, Charlie snapped the lunchbox to his chest.

Mr Clarke got close enough for Charlie to smell the designer body spray and bad breath. He growled through clenched teeth.

‘Listen, you ginger midget. You can either show what’s in the box, or I can take what’s in the box.’

Panic swept through Charlie. The voice in his head shouted over and over: *No No No No No No No No No No.* He closed his eyes tight, gripped the lunchbox, and got ready for the onslaught. Clarkie made a move for the lunchbox. Then nothing, just the sound of running feet.

'Charlie, is everything okay? Have you finished your lunch?' Mrs Lowther was walking close by. One of the henchmen had alerted the group and they scattered. Charlie was still shaking with fear. But at least he'd protected Dudley. That was something.

The bell went for the end of the lunch break and the usual herd galloped towards the doors. Charlie found a gap, joined the crowd, and got carried along. A few metres from the doors Charlie couldn't breathe. The pain in his side made him swing round. He'd been punched in the ribs.

CLARKIE!

Hiya Ginge. This isn't over. You owe me a lunchbox.' He beamed a huge smile.

Eight

An Appointment with Fear

Charlie went home beside himself with fear following the incident at the centre doors. He had never been bullied before and wasn't sure what was going on. Going over and over the incident, wondering if he'd done anything to provoke or offend Clarkie, only made things worse. The cold shivers grabbed him and he started to feel sick again.

He was glad to be going home to safety and comfort, the events of the day and Clarkie swept to the back of his mind somewhere.

'Hi, Mum!' Charlie bounced into the back seat of the car with his school bag and lunchbox.

'Wow, you're chirpy. Had a good day?' she enquired.

'Yeah. Today was brilliant. We had a quiz about countries of the world beginning with each letter of the alphabet.' The words raced from his mouth, almost without thinking.

'That's great.' She clunked the car into drive and they were on their way to the supermarket.

Charlie's gaze shot to his lunchbox as the lid popped open. Dudley shot him the sternest look and mouthed, 'Tell Mum what happened!' Dudley was gesturing with closed punching fists.

Charlie did a pointed ferret face and whispered, 'No, shhh!'

Back home, Dudley couldn't contain his frustration. He popped the lid of the lunchbox open, jumped out, and marched across the desk until he was nose to nose with a slumped Charlie.

'What's going on, Sir? Why wouldn't you tell Mum about Clarkie and what happened at school?' He waited. 'I hope you realise I was shaken around in there. I had just taken a bite of a Cheesy Puff then …

Do you know how difficult it is for a spider to get a Cheesy Puff out of his ear? Pretty flippin' difficult, I can tell you. Spiders aren't supposed to have Cheesy Puffs in their ears. If we were, I'm sure I would have read about it somewhere.'

His attempt to cheer his friend didn't work. The words just bounced around the silence.

Charlie raised his head for a moment. His eyes filled and tears poured down his cheeks as his shoulders started to jump. He dived back into his crossed arms, sobbing.

'Ohhhhh, mate.' Dudley raised himself on two legs and wrapped the remaining six around his friend. 'You have to tell Mum, Mrs Lowther or the Head Teacher. You have to tell someone.'

'I can't,' Charlie croaked. 'He hit a teacher at his other school. What would he do to me if I told anyone and got him in trouble? Look at what happened to Molly. If I stay out of his way I should be okay. I'm just being silly.'

Dudley wasn't so sure. 'I can't tell you what to do. But I think you should tell someone. You know I'll support you, whatever you choose to do, but you can't let him get away with this. I get that it's your choice. I'm here no matter what.'

Charlie flopped to the bed and fell asleep until Mum called.

'Charlie! Dinner! I've done your favourite.'

He didn't stir. Five minutes later, she called again.

'Charrrlllleeeeeeeeee! … Diiiiiiinnnerrrrrr!'

He didn't stir from the deep sleep he'd fallen into.

'CHARLIE ROBINSON! DINNER! NOW!' She was starting to lose patience. Growly Mum would be the next step.

He rolled over, folded his arms, and pulled his knees up, making himself into a ball. Dudley appeared from under the bed.

'Charlie, Mum's calling. You can't ignore her. She'll think something is wrong.'

He rolled back with a huge sigh, took a breath, and shouted, 'I'm not feeling very well, Mum!'

Tap ... tap. A soft knuckle knocked on the bedroom door.

'Sweetie, what's wrong? Can I come in?' she asked.

'No need, Mum, I'm okay. Had a little sleep and woke with a tummy ache. Just a case of the bottom burps.' *(Code for windy pops or farting.)*

'Are you sure?' she said, concerned.

'Yeah, I'm fine. I'll be down soon.' He tried to mask his sadness.

'Okay, don't be long. We've got Bolognese piadas. See you downstairs.'

Now it has to be said, Charlie's mum's Bolognese piadas are the stuff of legend and Charlie's absolute favourite food in the entire world. Even above chocolate, crisps, jelly snakes, and the legendary Cheesy Puffs!

Dad had taught Mum how to make Bolognese Piada Wraps when they were at university together. He said he came from a long line of Italian Robinsons and made the best Piadas ever. The reality was somewhat different.

Dad had learned to make the dish while on holiday in Italy when he was fourteen. He fancied the daughter of the restaurant owner where the family ate. He asked her out on a date, but her dad would only allow them to see each other if he worked in the kitchen for the two weeks of the holiday, to prove his respect for her and the family.

They could see each other during the day and he would work at the restaurant for a few hours at night. He would get to see Rosa, would show her dad respect, and he'd learn something about a restaurant too. Everyone was happy. Apparently it was worth it because Rosa was beautiful.

So, he learned how to construct dozens of meals with meat, cheese, salad, and folded wheat Frisbees. In return he got to argue with Rosa the Italian diva for two weeks. That's what really happened, according to Charlie's mum. Regardless of the tale Dad told.

Dad then bestowed his vast meat Frisbee knowledge on Mum. BUT! She apparently made them better, which annoyed Dad, a lot!

Grandma and Grandpa Robinson dropped the bombshell when they came to dinner once. It was Charlie's fourth birthday dinner, the year before the divorce. Mum suggested Dad cook the famous Piadas. He didn't think they were birthday food, so she did it. Grandma and Grandpa loved them. They said they were nicer than usual. They may have been sticking it to Dad because he refused to make them, but it stuck. That was how the monster was created.

Mum always told Dad she added a secret ingredient to the recipe, which made it her own. But when Charlie helped her make the dish once, she admitted there was nothing extra in there, with a wink, a finger to her lips, and a shush.

Charlie drifted off again, thinking about the piada story, but was startled awake by something being rammed in his ear. Confused, he reached up. Dudley was sitting on the bed in front of him.

‘By the way, there’s something I didn’t tell you about spiders. We do payback, BIG TIME!’ Dudley chuckled. ‘Come on, grumpy chops. These Piadas sound nice.’

Charlie looked at his hand. Dudley had stuck a Cheesy Puff in his ear while he dozed off. He couldn’t help but shake his head and smile.

Maybe things were not as bad as he thought.

Nine

Debts Paid with Jumping Spiders

Billy Clarke wasn't at school on Friday. Miss Merrick said he had a dentist's appointment and wouldn't be in.

Poor Sod. Charlie thought. *Let's hope he doesn't get the big needle right through his head and into his brain.*

A relieved Charlie sat comfortably in his seat, happy that Clarkie wasn't going to be at school. You could almost hear the sigh when Miss made the announcement. It meant peace. The kind of peace adults feel when a manager isn't at work. Mrs Robinson said they rejoiced at her office when a particular manager had flu or a serious illness.

Charlie looked across to Molly, who threw back her 'I've just won a prize' smile. She was obviously a happy bunny at the thought Clarkie might be in pain at the dentist.

The day before the weekend and school seemed to get back to how it used to be before the reign of Billy, or Bully Clarke, as he was becoming known.

Nobody had to watch out for a prowling Clarke followed by a trail of fake gangster wannabees dragging behind like so much noisy rubbish tied to the back of a wedding car.

Nobody looked over their shoulder, ready to make a swift exit to avoid any attention from his group. Nobody had to worry about hiding the little things they brought into school to make the playground a little more entertaining. They didn't have rush packed lunch or keep one eye on food and the other scouting for trouble from the bile of the bullies. It was going to be a good day.

The bullies seemed lost without their supreme leader. At lunchtime four members of the dark lord's entourage sat at the picnic benches by the back wall of the playground, looking lost. Like lions without a leader they watched everyone else running, bouncing, and laughing. There was confusion and a lack of focus without the boss, dark lord or big smelly cheese.

Ten minutes passed. Obviously overcome by temptation to flex their muscles, the front one leaned to his right and muttered to another, who passed it on to his neighbour, then the next, and so on. Until it came back to the left ear of the first one, who looked at the messenger as though he was mad. A nod and they stood in unison. They surveyed the herd slowly at first, looking for a stray or weak member.

A small ball bounced against the concrete fence that separated the school from the gardens of the local houses and rolled in their direction. A year four boy had followed the bouncing ball. Peter Joseph stopped it with his foot and picked it up.

'Is this yours?' he asked sarcastically, offering the ball back. The boy reached out, but as he did Peter Joseph pulled the ball away and laughed.

He looked over his shoulder as if to cue laughter from the group. They obliged, sniggering and snorting into their hands.

Peter Joseph had been an invisible child before joining the dark lord as a minion. He wasn't a flea bag or a horrible child. Rather, he was the kind of child whose name you wouldn't recognise on the register. The kind you would point to in class photographs and ask, 'Who's he?'

Peter, or Grandma Joseph as he was known to his classmates, was a rather ordinary child. Average height and build for his age, but with rather pointed ferrety features, insane unruly fox-brown hair, and an overall look that suggested he might be a soap dodger. He added to the look with jumper sleeves rolled up ten times so they didn't look like floppy socks at the end of his arms.

As if that wasn't bad enough he was followed by a cloud of something that sort of smelled like aftershave or body spray. But it definitely wasn't a good brand. Good brands don't have the vague waft of cat's wee in the background.

In year four, someone had said he smelled like a cat lady and it stuck. From that day on, he was known as Grandma Joseph and he hated it.

The mention of the name made him descend into a fit of temper. That amused the class. They laughed more and he got worse. It was never ending once it started. More often than not teachers had to stop it before Peter's little red face went pop.

Grandma Joseph seemed to enjoy being a minion of the dark lord. It gave him a sense of purpose and made him feel powerful. Clarkie came along at the right time for him – he enjoyed being a bully. It was obviously a way to pay back those who mocked him.

'Stop messing about. Can I have the ball?' the small boy enquired firmly.

'But you didn't say Pa-LEASE!' Grandma Joseph leaned forward for effect.

'Just gimmie the ball, Grandma!' he said with a sarcastic smirk and a demanding hand.

Grandma Joseph went from zero to rage in a heartbeat.

‘You want it? YOU WANT IT?’ He marched towards the concrete fence that bordered the local terraced houses.

‘Then go get it!’ He drew back his arm and threw the ball over the fence into a garden behind. Nothing ever came back from those gardens. It was a death sentence for anything that went over.

‘You git! Thanks a bunch!’ the small boy shouted as he stormed off to tell his friends about the fate of their ball.

Not much could be done about a lost ball. Children weren’t supposed to take them to school and were aware of what could happen. More often than not, balls were confiscated, burst, or lost. This one was put down as an angry loss by Grandma Joseph. The bile of bullies continued to circle the playground, looking for prey.

It wasn’t long before Grandma’s radar settled on Charlie, Molly, and Robert, enjoying a peaceful lunch at the picnic tables by the centre doors. Charlie was happy and relaxed, thinking about Clarkie and the possibility that the dentist had left him with the biggest needle sticking out of his neck.

The calm made them vulnerable.

Grandma Joseph and his band of not so merry men crept up behind Charlie. Confident with his new power he walked up close enough to touch Charlie’s back with his knees.

‘Hiya Ginge. Whatchya got there? Lunchbox?’ He cupped and rubbed his chin sarcastically. ‘Don’t you owe us a lunchbox?’

‘Yeah, Grandma. Want a sandwich?’ Charlie’s chuckle slapped him down in the same way he was always slapped down. On the other side of the bench, Molly and Robert bowed their heads and giggled into their lunch bags.

‘What did you call me … GINGE?’ Grandma descended into that raging place yet again.

Charlie was taken aback a little. Grandma wasn’t usually this aggressive. He continued with the sarcastic approach anyway.

‘Sorry, dearest Grandma Joseph. Would you like a sandwich? You probably couldn’t hear me because of the years of wax in your lugholes.’ Quite pleased with himself he leaned forward and laughed out loud. Molly and Robert joined in. As he did, Grandma Joseph grabbed his lunchbox.

Instinctively Charlie stopped and leapt off the bench. They were suddenly face to face like gunfighters in old Western films. The playground fell silent.

‘Okay, OKAY! I’m sorry. Please can I have my lunchbox back.’ He threw out a hand and gestured for Grandma to give him the lunchbox.

'What's in here that's so special, anyway?' Grandma raised the lunchbox up to eye level, paused, and then gave it an almighty shake.

'NOOOOOOOOOOOOOOOOOO!' Charlie shouted, certain that Dudley would be hurt, or killed.

Grandma raised the lunchbox to eye level again. Holding it in his left hand, he proceeded to open the lid with his right. Inside, there was a chicken and crisp sandwich that looked like road kill. Jelly snakes were roaming around, loose from the packet, and the bottom of the box was covered in a deep layer of Cheesy Puff crumbs.

Grandma laughed, turned, and showed his handiwork to his fellow dark minions. Suddenly there was movement in the Cheesy Puffs. He moved his face closer. Then suddenly … BOING!

Dudley and a cloud of Cheesy Puff crumbs flew out of the lunchbox, landing on Grandma's face. What happened next can only be described as hilarious.

Grandma flung the lunchbox and shrieked as loud as his lungs would allow.

'GET IT OFF! GET IT OFF! GET IT OFF!'

In a manic attempt to grab Dudley he spun around in a whirr, hitting himself in the face. He randomly jumped around, madly rubbing his hair as if he was shampooing in the shower of the crazy, the whole time screeching like an insane thing from a horror movie.

The not so dark minions scattered. Grandma ran crying to Mrs Lowther who couldn't breathe she was laughing so hard. She was crying when he got to her.

'MISS! MISS! PLEASE GET IT OFF! … SPI-DER! SPIDER! SPIDER!' Begging her, he frantically gestured to his head.

Wiping her eyes, she calmed herself and reassured him.

'It's gone. Don't worry.'

'Are you sure? I can feel it on me.' He shrugged and rubbed his hair again.

'I promise. It's gone. Now go to registration. The bell has gone,' she said.

Charlie, Robert, and Molly had already made their way to the doors, trying to catch their breath as they went. Charlie scooped up the remains of his lunch and dumped it in the lunchbox. A black fuzzy leg emerged from a pile of Cheesy Puffs in the corner. The hand on the end threw up a thumb in acknowledgement.

Relieved, he closed the lunchbox. He went to afternoon registration happy that Dudley had scored one for the little bloke, against the bullies.

BOING!
GET IT OFF
GET IT OFF!
GET IT OFF!

Ten

Shaken. Not Stirred

On Friday afternoon Charlie bounced out of school, still laughing to himself about the events at lunchtime. Mum swung the car door open as he approached and he jumped in, giggling and waving his arms about.

'Get it off … ha, ha, ha … Get it off!'

'Good afternoon, Mr Robinson. You seem chipper. Had a good day?' Mum enquired.

'Yep.' He chuckled. 'Had a great day.'

'Good.' She smiled. 'Don't forget your belt, Sir.'

'On it, Mum,' he replied with a warm efficiency.

Clunk! The car jumped into gear and they were off, Charlie still making funny faces and rubbing his head.

Two streets from the school Mum asked, 'My gorgeous son, can I ask? Do you fancy a date night with your mum tonight? There's free pizza and the new superhero movie in it for you.'

Charlie put on his concentration face and rubbed his chin before answering. Mum laughed and stared at him in the rear view mirror. 'Excuse me, Sir. Don't think too long and hard. It's only dinner and a movie with the hottest mum on the planet.'

'Just checking my diary for a window; won't be a second.' Charlie took his maths book from his school bag and flicked the pages as though looking through a diary.

'Oh really?' said Mum in her fake offended voice.

Charlie's eyes settled on a page in the fake diary. He pointed and nodded to himself. 'Yep. It's okay, I have time this evening. But on one condition.'

'And that is?' she asked.

'My spider with an artificial leg can come too?' he insisted.

Mum did her 'Hmmm' face. 'Okay. It's a date then. I'll pick you up about six o'clock?'

'It's a date. See you then.' Charlie pretended to write the date in his maths book.

They turned on to the A339 to Basingstoke. Popcorn and drinks had just been added to the weekly shopping list. Mum found her favourite album on the phone, got into soul diva character, cleared her throat, and gave her all-time favourite song some serious welly – '*And IIIII was borrrn in Georgia ...* ' When, in fact Charlotte was actually born in Brentwood, Essex.

Movement from the lunchbox on the seat caught Charlie's eye. Dudley cracked open the lid and was clearly annoyed. Legs were flailing around like a dyspraxic windmill in a blur of black fuzz. Charlie tried to make sense of the sign language but wasn't doing very well.

Dudley closed the lid in frustration. A few minutes later he popped up again with a crumpled napkin, pointing frantically at words he'd scrawled with a Cheesy Puff.

He seemed concerned that Charlie had outed him. He mouthed angrily.

'What are you doing? You can't tell Mum about me.'

Charlie shushed him, looked forward to see if Mum had noticed the commotion, and closed the lunchbox. Dudley was already out and on his shoulder.

'You can't tell Mum about me!' he grumbled through his beard into Charlie's left ear.

'BAHHHH!' Charlie jumped.

Mum noticed the noise mid-chorus but didn't miss a beat. '*Will You Still Love Me Tooooo-morrrow.* Everything okay, sweetie?'

'Yeah, nothing to worry about. Just got scared by my spider with an artificial leg, hehe.' Dudley almost fainted off his shoulder, but Charlie had stumbled on a way of hiding Dudley in plain sight. He reckoned he could say pretty much anything about anything at times like this. Mum was doing that thing parents do, when they don't listen to a word while pretending to pay attention to everything.

Charlie decided to test his theory.

'Muuum?' The tone phrased the question to come.

'*Youuu say that I'm the onnnly wuunnnn* ... yes, dear?' There was no way this would register while she was in mid-song.

'Is it okay if I bring my gi-nor-moose spider friend named Dudley to the cinema and for pizza with us?' He threw it out there, turned his ear towards the front seat, and waited …

'Yeah, that's great sweetie. I'm looking forward to it too … *So tell me now, and I won't ask again ... la la la'*

Nothing. *Ha-ha*! This could be very interesting.

They arrived home, having hit the aisles at Sainsbury's. Dudley wanted a chat. He'd been kicking the inside of the lunchbox the whole journey home but Charlie sat on it. He walked over to the desk in his bedroom, carefully placed the lunchbox next to the computer, and waited.

The catch clicked, and the lid raised slowly. A huge frown emerged before the spider did. Like an annoyed Grandma he had two legs folded in front. He stood up on the remaining five, tapping out his frustration on the inside of the box with the artificial one.

Covered in orange Cheesy Puff crumbs, he was not happy.

Charlie broke the silence. He looked wide eyed at Dudley, raised his hands palms up, and said,

'What? I can talk about you now. We haven't got to be careful and hide you away. Mum thinks I've got an imaginary friend or something.'

The spider loosened his crossed arms. His mouth did that funny side to side thing people do when they're thinking. His frown retreated back into his face.

'I trust you not to get me killed, Sir. Or worse, fall into the hands of the government for scientific experiments, because they do that, you know. I've seen the films.'

Charlie stood and placed his left hand over the right side of his chest. 'I promise,' he said solemnly.

'That's the wrong side,' Dudley said, shaking his head. 'Your heart is on the other side.'

Charlie quickly changed sides.

'I promise, Sir. I will protect you with my life. Because you are the bestest friend I ever had and I love you.'

Dudley's eyes became wide and filled up. His face relaxed and a tear squeezed out but hung desperately to his eyelid. He gazed warmly at his friend.

'Right! I have to get ready. I've got a hot date. See ya later, mate.' He spun round and whizzed out of the room before the words had finished leaving his mouth.

Dudley flopped into the pile of cheesy crumbs, which puffed up and danced in the air around him. He leaned over the side of the lunchbox, sighed, and poked out his tongue to catch the cheesy goodness.

'Yeah. I love you too. I actually do.'

Eleven

Crouch, Bind, Saturday

On Saturday morning, Charlie woke with a serious case of the farts and a mouth like a tramp's beard. Mum had let him take the leftover pizza to his room after their date and he had the dreaded pepperoni hangover. It may have been a mistake to have two slices before falling asleep.

A rustling from the desk caught his attention. He jumped up to investigate. On closer inspection, it was coming from the pizza box. Raising a copy of *The BFG* above his head he carefully lifted the lid, ready to bash the first thing he saw. Until he saw what he saw. A vision burned on his memory forever. A sight so hideous he would gladly have jumped inside his own head and washed his brain.

A huge jet black mountain rose up on long black furry trunks among the pepperoni slices. It turned and fixed Charlie with its terrifying steely glare.

'Sorry, I got hungry and let's not

forget you abandoned me.' Semi-apologetic Dudley stood in front of him with peppers in his beard and cheesy pepperoni hanging out of his mouth.

'You almost got bashed by *The BFG*,' Charlie said.

Between chews Dudley found some words. 'Yeahhhh, that's never a good thing.' He giggled. 'What's the plan for today, Sir?'

Charlie squinted a thoughtful squint before replying. 'Probably shopping again. Mum said we're out for the whole day today. That usually means shopping for school or work stuff. She's going to tell me this morning.'

'Char-leeeee. Are you up?' Mum called upstairs.

Charlie echoed back. 'Yeah, Mum, just getting up now.'

'Can you come down, please? We can't have a conversation down the hallway.' Mum didn't like those shouting conversations that often take place between people in different parts of the house. Like the toilet–kitchen chat or the kitchen–bedroom chat that always ended with the 'I'm not having a conversation down the hallway' comment.

'Be back in a sec.' He left Dudley to finish the pepperoni he'd started a few minutes earlier. Apparently spiders' teeth were not suited to chewing pepperoni, so it was taking some time. Charlie didn't mind. At least it shut the spider up.

He did the usual bounce down six stairs, then jumped six stairs. He got warned by Mum to 'Not Do That!' He apologised as usual, and then …

'Sweetie.' What usually followed was not good when Mum started a sentence with '*Sweetie*'. 'You like rugby, don't you?' she enquired.

'Yes. Whyyyy?' He batted it back cautiously.

'Well … a partner at the practice has a director's box at the Twickenham Stoop and has offered it to us because he has to go to France on business today. Quins are playing my Chiefies. All we have to do is get there. Do you fancy it?' She produced a card from her bag and waved it expectantly.

Chiefies meant the Exeter Chiefs. She had been a fan for a few years. It started while she was dating Gavin, a man with fewer brain cells than feet. Gavin said he was once an amateur player who could have signed professionally, but didn't because his career came first. Being a professional idiot obviously took more commitment than rugby.

Charlie didn't believe a word of it. Gavin was a man lacking the coordination necessary to turn around without falling down. He also complained a lot! If he banged his elbow in the car, he whined like a baby. If he bumped his hand at home, he complained no end. But the worst was when he cut his hand chopping onions. It was a small cut that oozed a bit of blood but he made enough noise for the people in the next village to hear. Definitely more football than rugby player, Charlie thought.

Mum and Gavin lasted about three months. And that was three months too long, in Charlie's opinion.

Mum had two favourite players. Thomas 'the Tank' Waldrom, a monster of a man who liked playing skittles with opposition players; and her absolute favourite was '*her Henry'*, or Henry Slade, the Chiefs' fly half.

Henry had once kissed Mum on the cheek when he signed her match programme and took a selfie with her. She was smitten from that moment, but only because she respected his commitment to the game. Of course!

'Wooo hoo, yes, please,' shouted a delighted Charlie. 'Should I get ready now?'

'Might be an idea. We have a parking space booked, so we're driving up to London,' Mum informed him.

Charlie climbed the stairs two at a time, raced down the hall, and back into the bedroom. He scanned. Dudley wasn't anywhere obvious. He looked in the pizza box … No. Book shelf … No. Lunchbox … No. 'Under the bed!' he said to himself. He jumped on the bed, leaned over, and whipped up the dangling duvet.

'Shhhhhhhhh!' Dudley cut through what Charlie was about to say. Poised on five tiptoes with hands together, he was almost ready to throw his booted artificial leg at a rugby ball he had liberated from Mum's keyring. Three feet away stood two red and black Friendly Dragon chopsticks with a red striped straw across. The whole thing was stuck to the floor with Blu-Tac, pinched from Charlie's desk drawer.

The spider had constructed some rugby posts.

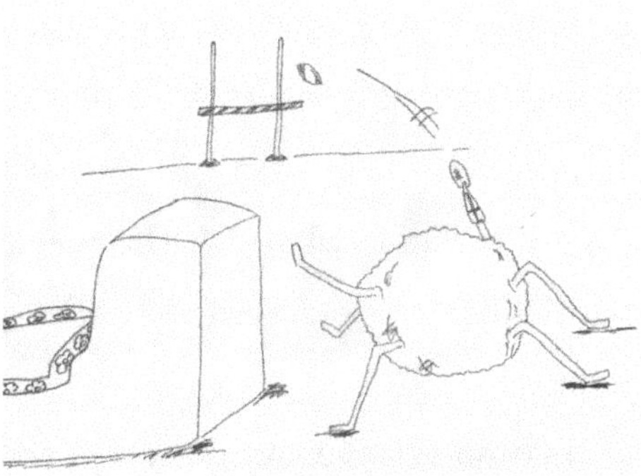

THUD! 'YES!' Dudley slotted the kick between the posts. 'Still got it, just like Johnny,' he boasted. 'So, my friend; My dearest most wonderful friend in the whole wide world. Are we all attending the Quins versus Chiefs match this afternoon?' He beamed a huge toothy smile and batted his eyelids.

'Err, yes, and how did you know?' Charlie was a little puzzled.

'Well, Sir. Some of us actually take notice when your mum is on the phone. I listened when her boss called earlier. And thank you,' the spider replied.

The pair readied themselves. After a quick visit to the shop for drinks, crisps, and chewing gum they were ready to set off. The journey was an hour and a half of hell. Dudley would not SHUT UP! Charlie was seriously considering turning him inside out if he heard 'are we there yet?' one more time.

Charlie tried everything to keep him amused. He had brought the tiny playing cards from last year's Christmas crackers, so they could play cards. But the spider complained when he lost and then starting cheating. He brought Travel Connect 4 but the spider ate three of the counters. Dudley wasn't even satisfied by the constant supply of Jaffa Cakes. Charlie was starting to understand why Mum got annoyed when he was a pest on long journeys.

Just outside Twickenham, Charlie had had enough of the moaning Jaffa Cake monster and gave in to his frustration. In mid-complaint he grabbed the spider, stuffed him in a coat pocket, and snapped the popper closed.

Ahhh, peace at last! he thought.

Aside from Mum getting her diva on, there was quiet in the car for about ten minutes. Then three legs and a scrunched up ball of paper emerged from the corner of the pocket. Charlie smoothed the paper ball and tried to decipher the writing, which seemed to be written in chocolate spit. The note had been scratched on a tissue.

SEND HELP AND JAFFA CAKES!
KIDNAPPED IN COAT POCKET!

Charlie smiled, took a bite from a Jaffa Cake, and slipped it into his pocket. They arrived at the gates of the Stoop. Mum showed her pass and they found their parking space.

The directors' box was amazing! It was about the size of a big living room. Opposite the entrance, huge sliding glass doors opened on to twenty or so private seats which had the best view of the pitch from side to side.

Three waiters and a manager looked after Mum and Charlie's every need. Huge piles of food decorated the massive table along the back wall, which had endless supplies of glistening meats and veggies at one end. In the middle were mountains of Yorkshire puddings with shiny brown crispy potatoes and, at the far end, four large silver trays covered with swirling pastries, cakes, and the most luxurious chocolate things.

Next to the table were two huge fridges, crammed with rows of every drink imaginable. Eight different types of water, every fruit juice known, more wine than they have in France, and the most expensive Champagne in the world.

The huge round table in the centre of the room was set for dinner. Charlie and Mum were invited to sit. Napkins were placed in their laps and non-stop food arrived for half an hour before kick-off. Charlie dived in, occasionally sneaking handfuls of chicken, potatoes, veggies, and a slab of chocolate fudge cake to the spider hiding under his coat on the next chair.

Ten minutes before kick-off and they were stuffed. Young Mr Robinson politely put his knife and fork together and placed them on his plate. He leaned back in his chair and made one of those noises people usually make after Christmas dinner.

While Mum wasn't looking he leaned down and pulled back his coat. Dudley was on his back with all eight legs spread out, surrounded by crumbs and covered in chocolate shavings. It seemed they had all eaten to bursting.

The crowd started to get noisy, which usually meant the game was about to start. Charlie slid the heavy glass door left and the cold rushed in as the pair stepped out of their private restaurant into the stadium to take their seats. Mum nudged Charlie as the teams ran out onto the pitch, pointing to '*her Henry'*. Dudley peeked out from Mum's scarf piled on the next seat. He gave a mad 'thumbs up' as the referee blew his whistle for kick-off.

It was a fairly one-sided game. Quins were not on top form. There wasn't much to cheer, apart from Thomas the

Tank having a try disallowed and Mum's Henry scoring a try and two penalties.

Charlie decided to take Mum down a peg and even the score. She was way too smug about '*her Henry*'.

'Oh dear. Now Thomas just looks like a fat bloke with a ball jumping up in the air.' He chuckled at his own joke which made the waiter giggle and look down.

The box next door was owned by the insurance company Havia. They didn't have guests because they'd been let down by a Japanese company due to watch the game. So an endless stream of orange-faced ladies dressed in blue and yellow marched back and forth urgently, looking for jobs to do. They were the orange-faced smiley Public Relations ladies.

The marching became more frantic as the game approached the final whistle. Charlie heard them chirping louder and louder, accompanied by lots of hand waving and more frantic marching. Eventually one of the smiley oranges knocked on the glass window separating the boxes. She pointed at Mr Robinson and mouthed, 'Would you like to present the Man of the Match award, young man?'

One of the Japanese guests had been due to present the Man of the Match award, live on the ESPN Sports TV channel. They desperately needed a replacement, so they asked Charlie.

He looked at Mum, who nodded enthusiastically. ‘Go for it,’ she said.

The orange lady beckoned the pair as the huge glass divide swished open. Charlie scooped up the spider and they were escorted to the club shop.

Charlie felt really important. The orange ladies gave him a club shirt and a bag of goodies. Dudley jumped out of his pocket and into the goody bag where he found a tiny rugby ball and managed to get his legs stuck in a mascot shirt for the car. He rustled the bag to get Charlie’s attention.

‘Pssst! Does my bum look big in this?’ He giggled before falling back into the pile of goodies.

The orange ladies kicked into high gear, whisking the pair down the players’ tunnel and on to the pitch, where Charlie was given a large cold yellow bottle of Champagne, as big as his head and twice as heavy. This was the Man of the Match award.

ESPN TV cameramen walked around busily, trying to find a good spot to film the presentation. They trailed thick cables everywhere, which were picked up and bunched together by spotty teenage assistants.

Charlie started to get nervous and looked over to Mum for support. She wasn’t much help. The insane smile and ‘thumbs up’ stopped being magic by the age of five. Obviously she didn’t get the memo. He was brought into shot by one of the smiley orange people so they could check the light, which seemed bright enough.

The Man of the Match was interviewed and Charlie was invited to hand over the head-sized bottle of Champers.

It was Mum's Henry!

Behind the camera she bounced up and down, clapping her hands. Charlie carefully presented the bottle, shook Henry's hand, and stepped back.

Interview over, Charlie and Mum turned and started to walk back towards the players' tunnel with the orange smiley ladies.

'Excuse me. Charlie's Mum?' They stopped and turned around. Henry Slade had followed them off the pitch. 'Charlie tells me that you're my number one fan, but you can't get down to Exeter that often?' he said.

'That's true.' Flustered Mum looked like she wanted to hide in her own shirt. She stepped behind Charlie and placed her hands on his shoulders.

'Can I give you a little something as a thank you for your support?' He held out the Man of the Match Champagne. 'Have you got a pen? Who should I sign it to?'

'Ch-Charlotte. Thank you.' She reached into her pocket and handed over a marker. Henry scribbled: *'To my number one fan Charlotte. Great to see you and Charlie today. Hope to see you at Exeter soon. Love Henry xx.'*

He handed the pen and the Champagne to her. As he handed it to her he leaned in and kissed her on the cheek.

'Look after Mum, Charlie. You only get one Mum. Hope to see you guys soon.' He turned and jogged down the tunnel, the number 10 on his shirt gradually enveloped in shadow.

Mum was gobsmacked. A jumble of incoherent rubbish came out for hours after, when she opened her mouth. Normally intelligent and feisty Mum had been replaced by someone who had their brain shook up.

She didn't make any sense until halfway home. They stopped at traffic lights, she reached for her bottle of Champagne, raised it to her lips and gave it the biggest kiss.

'Mwwwwah! My Henry,' she said with a huge smile.

Twelve

Robert the Brave

Time flies when you're famous and on TV, as Charlie realised when Monday came around again. Somebody pressed the treadmill button. He was ejected from bed and into school clothes, in much the same way as superheroes pull a library book or spin around in revolving doors, emerging dressed and ready for action. Charlie wasn't ready for action, because he had a real nemesis to be concerned about. The Dark Clarkie.

Time seemed to slip through his fingers, in super-fast motion like the old black and white films where people walked around at twice the speed. His bag and lunchbox packed themselves. Hair and teeth were brushed in a bathroom haze and before he knew it he was dressed and sitting at the breakfast bar in the kitchen.

Dudley snapped him back from the fuzzy place in his head. Tickling his left nostril with a furry foot, he shouted, 'Hello Hello. Anyone home? Earth calling Charlie!'

‘Sorry.’ Charlie sighed as he slumped over.

‘What’s up, Sir?’ Dudley was worried.

‘Oh, nothing. It’s just that the weekend goes too fast.’ He heaved a massive sigh.

In an attempt to lighten the mood, Dudley threaded three honey hoops on each of his front legs and started to twirl them. Unmoved, Charlie flopped onto the counter, chin in hands.

‘Uh-hum!’ He nodded towards each leg. ‘I could have been a circus spider you know. *Dat-dat duddle-duddle dat-dat daa-dat.*’ It didn’t work. ‘Is this because of that nasty Clarkie?’ he asked.

‘Naaa. Just don’t want to go back to school. I hate school.’ Charlie thumped the table with his fist.

Mum glided into the kitchen, wafting her arms.

‘*Aaaaaat laaaaaaast. My looooove has come alllong*!’ Etta James songs were getting a serious hammering this morning. Meeting ‘*her Henry*’ had made her quite mad. Normal Mum had been replaced by a whirlwind with a crush that occasionally popped out an arm to grab something from the cupboard or fridge.

Eventually the flurry of papers, sandwiches, and clothes came to rest in front of Charlie.

‘Ready?’ she enquired with raised eyebrows, ushering him towards the front door with her palms before he could answer. She stopped briefly to admire her Henry-kissed face in the hallway mirror, swished the scarf around her neck, and followed Charlie out. He was convinced she would have framed her face if she could.

The journey to school was more like a journey to the gallows. Charlie had drums in his head. Every set of traffic lights was a step closer to the doom named Clarkie. Only the cabbage throwing hostile crowd was missing. Not a great way to start the week after such a great weekend.

'Seeya later, sausage.' Mum blew a kiss as he reluctantly closed the car door. She was way too cheerful today.

Overseen by the flaky black gargoyles on the school gates, he drudged through the doors, down the corridor, and into class. He dropped onto his chair next to Robert and did his best to look unfazed by the cackling from Clarkie's group on the other side of the classroom. Grandma Joseph jumped up and down rubbing his head, recalling Friday's meeting with Dudley.

'Charlie?' Robert enquired.

'What?' Charlie replied.

'Can I ask you something?' he said.

'Go ahead.' Charlie sighed and leaned back in his seat.

'How did you get on TV on Saturday? I was watching rugby on ESPN and at the end you were there, giving Henry Slade his Man of the Match award.'

Charlie had forgotten the match was live on TV.

He sat up. ‘Errr. They asked me to do it. Mum and I were at the game and the smiling orange ladies asked me to present the award.’ He couldn’t help but be proud that he was a little bit famous. A rumble went round the class. It seemed most people had watched the game.

Even Miss Merrick had watched. She wasn’t a big rugby fan, but had a five-pound bet with her brother and had to watch. A bet she won.

This must be how famous people feel, Charlie thought.

The class rumble faded to silence and Miss Merrick called the register.

‘Megan Apsey …Donna Attwood …Connor Bagnoffit…’ Charlie looked around. Miss was getting close to Clarke and he wasn’t in. Monday might not be so horrendous after all. Famous and Billy Clarke wasn’t in. Seemed like Christmas.

It wasn’t to be. The door squeaked open and he waltzed in – just as Miss Merrick called his name.

‘Billy Clarke …’ No reply. He plopped onto his chair and oozed under the desk up to his chest. Blond arrogance was smeared all over his face, as usual.

‘BILLY CLARKE?’ Miss Merrick turned the volume up. He stared at her but still didn’t reply.

‘Are you here, young man?’ She stared at him over her glasses.

'Does it look like I'm here?' The insult tripped off his tongue comfortably. The real Clarkie wasn't just in the playground now. He'd come to class.

Miss Merrick huffed past the incident, looked down, and continued with a flick of her pen. Billy Clarke didn't intimidate her. She'd seen it all in her career.

She got into the Ds today, without any problem. Then, 'Shane Ditherchild!' Flick … Whoosh … BANG! Today's first pen took off across the room like a missile. As usual, she reached for another without breaking stride. She didn't notice it spearing a picture of the head teacher on the noticeboard next to the door.

'You should get that fixed, M-M-Miss. You could k-k-k-kill someone.' Young Clarkie mocked and laughed. His disciples joined the initial ripple, which built to a full-on chorus of giggles. Calmly, Miss Merrick stood up and walked towards the door. She turned the handle and wafted out.

'Well done, Clarkie. Now you've upset Miss.' Robert appeared angry. The giggles were instantly replaced by an endless silence. Nobody was sure what would happen next.

Clarkie sat up. 'Are we Miss's best friend now? Ya big tree.' A ripple from his group accompanied a screech as he pushed his chair backwards. He marched towards Robert and Charlie.

'Oh, look. Mr Famous is being protected by his girlfriend. And how is the famous ginger midget today? What's for lunch … MIDGET!' He bounced around in front of them. Everyone wondered what would happen next.

Charlie tried to look unafraid of the intimidating antics. 'You'd better sit down. Miss Merrick will be back in a minute.'

'Oh, yeah! Ya think the old bat scares me? Let her come back. Bring the old vampire on!' He bent his knees and held his arms out wide to look threatening, the way people do when they're looking for a fight.

Robert moved his lunch bag under the table. It caught Clarkie's attention.

'Oooh. What ya got today, Stretch? Anything nice for me?' He grabbed Robert's lunch and started to open the bag.

'Leave it!' Robert grabbed at the bag.

Charlie backed up his friend. 'Put it down!' he shouted.

The pair wrestled over the bag. It twisted this way and that as they spun around in a tug of war. They went forward, backwards, around in circles, bumping into desks, book cases, and the blackboard. They knocked all the pens off Miss Merrick's desk as the angry dance got faster and faster. Then the stitching tore on the little blue lunch bag and a bottle of frozen water flew out.

Then the stitching tore on the little blue lunch bag and a bottle of frozen water flew out.

CRASH! … It was over.

They both flew back as the bag gave way. Robert crawled out from under a desk and stood up. One side of his face was wet and shiny red. Clarkie had a big streak of red down the left side of his designer white shirt.

Stunned silence followed as everyone tried to make sense of what happened. Clarkie spoke first.

'You're a dead man! Look what you've done to my shirt.'

Robert staggered to the nearest seat and flopped down, dazed and confused. He touched his face and started to sob as it became clear he had cut his head.

Miss Merrick hovered back into the classroom and quickly assessed the situation. She whisked Robert to the medical room then went back to class to get some information.

'Can somebody please tell me what on earth happened here?'

‘Yes, Miss,’ Clarkie piped up. ‘Robert got up to sharpen a pencil and slipped. He hit his head on the corner of your desk,’ he said, pointing. ‘I tried to help,’ he continued. ‘Is he going to be okay, Miss? Is there anything we can do for him? I hope he’s okay.’

‘I’m sure he’ll be fine. He’s in good hands.’ She picked up the mess on the floor and placed it back on the desk, then turned to put books back on the shelf behind her.

As she turned, Clarkie glared at Charlie, grinned like a monster and mouthed, ‘You’re next, Superstar.’

Thirteen

Hide and … Swim Mate!

Charlie did his best to stay in class at break and lunchtime, after the incident in the classroom. He worked slower in class, so worksheets had to be finished off. It was all he could think of to stay away from Clarkie and his dark minions.

Miss Merrick was impressed at his commitment to sound waves and the structure of the ear. She didn't see the world beyond teaching. No teacher did. They saw school as a workplace and a place where children learned the things that would take them further in life. Most kids saw the school as another place: where the law of the playground took over twice a day.

Charlie sat at his worn wooden desk, studying the stained, gouged, cracked honey. He gently ran his fingers over the poked and scratched statements of previous occupants, wondering who they were and if they had the same problems he did. Their story would be stamped there forever, or at least until the school invested in some new desks.

Miss Merrick told the class that Robert had gone to hospital and received eight stitches in the cut above his eye.

She said he had a huge black eye and wouldn't be at school for a week.

Molly and Bethany found themselves work, helping the dinner ladies set up the lunch room during break time and helped with clearing up after lunch. Nathan started attending chess club, even though he didn't like the game and couldn't play chess. It seemed the group of friends were doing their best to stay out of the way and under Clarkie's radar.

Settled into their respective hiding places they had some safety. But it couldn't stay that way forever.

Thursday the tenth of November was a crunchy, frosty day; the perfect day to start year five swimming sessions. It didn't matter that the nearest river was ten miles away and that nobody in the village had a pond in their garden. Kids still needed to learn to save one of those black rubber bricks from the bottom of a swimming pool.

The school had invested in a small coach for each class of twenty-five to visit the county swimming pool in Basingstoke, about twelve miles away. Today 5M had to brave sub-zero temperatures to save the same family of black rubber bricks that had fallen into the pool again.

Charlie looked forward to swimming. It was a departure from reading his desk and having to pretend to be slower than he actually was. He didn't like pretending to be stupid. A smart cookie, he resented having to hide in the classroom, pretending to do work he could have completed hours before. But getting beaten to a pulp by the school overlord wasn't an attractive prospect either.

Miss Merrick called the afternoon register. Molly collected up the missiles and the class gathered their swimming kit together for the journey. Amid the clattering chairs and rumble of movement Charlie noticed Billy Clarke didn't seem comfortable that he was going to the pool. He was unusually quiet. The usual noise machine filed out of the classroom with everyone else, silent. He got on the coach and took his seat by the window at the back quietly.

As the coach set off, he stared blankly out of the window. It wasn't right. The dark lord of the classroom, Miss Merrick's menace, the pest of the playground, did not sit quietly. The horrible noisy git did anything but sit quietly.

Charlie guessed he hated swimming. Maybe he couldn't swim and would get dragged down to his end by a family of ferocious rubber bricks. Perhaps he'd get sucked down the filter on the bottom, minced into sausage, and whir around the machine forever.

Halfway to the pool, Charlie looked down at his drawstring bag and noticed a familiar fuzzy black leg sticking out from the centre of his rolled-up towel. He reached in with his index finger and poked. The leg withdrew.

The towel wobbled about a bit then stopped. A pair of black fuzzy eyebrows appeared, followed by glasses. Dudley looked up.

'You left a leg sticking out,' Charlie whispered.

'Whoops,' the spider said, chuckling to himself. 'Sorry about that.'

The half hour journey passed quickly. Having a secret spider for company made the journey more entertaining. Now and then the others asked Charlie why he laughed to himself so much. He simply shrugged his shoulders, smiled, and they went back to their conversations.

The children jostled for position as they got off the coach. Being first in line meant getting the best place in the changing room. Nobody wanted to be last in and as a result have to change in the cubicle without a door, or worse, the cubicle with a door that wouldn't close, which kept exposing your bum and hit you as it swung open.

Miss Merrick glided through the chlorine waft as she did a big entrance to the pool. Like a vampire on a skateboard she floated to the ticket window, where a young girl sat jingling a neck full of keys and a whistle. She did a head count, signed a piece of paper, and the class were free to break ranks and pile through to the changing rooms.

Charlie was expecting Clarkie to be a nightmare. But he wasn't. He found a single cubicle, changed into his swimming shorts quickly, went out to poolside and waited with everyone else: SILENT!

Charlie found his own cubicle. He pulled his towel from his drawstring bag, which unrolled and dumped the dizzy spider on the bench. He tried to stand but couldn't, wobbling and falling on tangled legs.

'Where are you going to go while I'm swimming?' Charlie enquired.

'I thought I'd have a look around. Don't worry. I'll stay out of sight. I'll see you back here when the class is over.' He jumped from the bench, and scurried around the walls to the open door leading to the pool. He turned. 'By the way. Please don't rescue Clarkie if he gets into trouble. The world would be a better place without him.' With that he disappeared around the corner.

Charlie joined the rest of the class and awaited instructions.

Dudley made his way along the wall towards the public viewing area, keeping an eye out to make sure he wasn't noticed. He made it to footbath between the pool and the changing rooms.

'G'day, mate.' The voice made him almost jump out of his fuzzy skin.

'Haven't seen you here before, mate. Where ya from?'

In front of him was a spider half his size with wet, slicked-back, blond hair. He had an orange flip-flop on each foot, wore a bright red lace around neck with keys and a whistle which covered a vest that said:

AUSSIE SPIDERS

DO IT

EIGHT TIMES BETTER!

He carried a long pole with a hook at the end, made from two pencils, a clothes hanger, and a lot of Sellotape. 'Just visiting, mate?' he asked.

'Err … yes, Sir.' Dudley hesitated. He hadn't expected to see anyone while he was sneaking around.

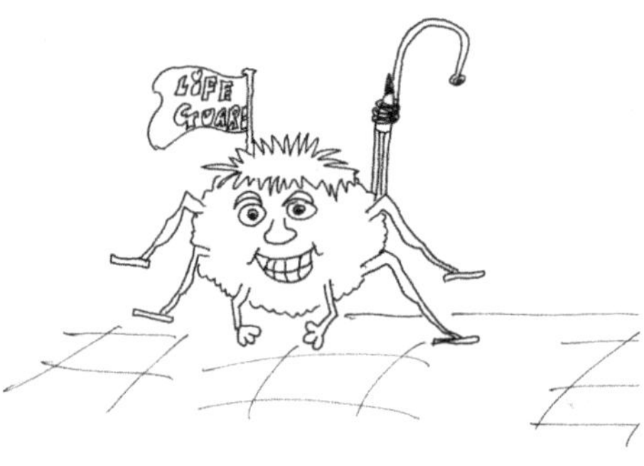

'Name's Aubrey, mate. Aubrey Grainger. Former one hundred centimetre Olympic freestyle sprint champ and world record holder. Came to the UK for the World Swimming Champs last year. Team went home without me. Decided to stick around. Pleased to meet ya! Got a name?'

'Clump. Dudley Clump. Pleased to meet you, Sir.' Dudley held out a leg which Aubrey grabbed and shook strongly.

'Fancy a brew, mate?' He turned and gestured for Dudley to follow. They rounded the wall towards the offices. He casually rescued a woodlouse and an earwig that had fallen into the footbath and they squeezed under the door and into the admin office.

Aubrey had set up home here. Dudley followed as he rounded the filing cabinet and squeezed through a gap in the wall, which opened out into the most luxurious office and living area. To the left were a doll's house wood-effect desk and a working lamp. Behind, on the wall, Aubrey had a chart with a list of his rescues over three months.

At the back of the room the kitchen area had tiny wooden cupboards, a working kettle, and a battery operated washing machine. The cooker used two small light bulbs to heat food and the sink had running water too.

On the right Aubrey's bedroom area looked comfortable. The action hero duvet and pillow set were lit by a lamp on a bedside drawer set. At the front of the room, on the right, a long sofa and small table sat opposite his desk. The whole area looked a little odd, decorated in strips of coloured copier paper dotted with miniature works of art. On the floor, a square of mustard coloured office carpet with a frayed corner took pride of place.

Aubrey had appointed himself resident lifeguard for the insects and small mini beasts that fell into the footbath. He had lived at the swimming pool since his team went back to Australia.

'Where did you get all this stuff?' a quizzical Dudley asked.

'Easy, mate. There's a kids group on the second floor of the building. They used to have a fully furnished doll's house. They don't anymore.' He chuckled.

Aubrey made Dudley a cup of tea and the two chatted while 5M did their thing in the pool. Dudley told the story of the scrum injury which led to him having an artificial leg and about the Secret Spider facility at Daniel Craig's house. In return Aubrey explained that he was universally hated by his team because he was always so upbeat and enthusiastic. That was why the team left him in England.

Dudley told Aubrey about Charlie and how they'd met. He explained how his best friend was being terrorised by Clarkie and his bile of bullies, and Aubrey said Dudley shouldn't hesitate to ask if either of them needed his help.

The pair arrived back at poolside shortly before Charlie and the class got out. Dudley had never seen Charlie swim and was impressed as he cut through the water like a dolphin and swooped down to get his brick.

The goggled redhead popped up with his prize. He thrust the large black rubber brick into the air. Like a proud dad, Dudley puffed out his chest and smiled to Aubrey.

As Charlie suspected, Billy Clarke was not at home in the water. In fact, he hated it. While the rest of the class splashed around like caught fish Clarkie hugged the side rail, wincing every time he was splashed. There was a chink in the bully's armour.

Dudley had an idea.

'Aubrey? Have you got a minute, mate?'

Fourteen

Weapons of Miss Destruction

The swimming session was over and a family of bricks had been saved and returned to their home. 5M went to get changed then met Miss Merrick at the meeting area by the ticket office. She arrived and did a quick head count as she did her vampire on a skateboard thing towards the main doors. The warm air whooshed out as she flung them open, replaced by an icy blast that chilled damp skin and brought everyone out in goosebumps.

CRUNCH, CRUNCH, CRUNCH!

Miss Merrick got three steps before the class had proof she wasn't a vampire after all. She left footprints.

The roar went up. IT HAD SNOWED!

Discipline went out of the window as the snowfall registered. The class broke ranks to scoop up piles of crunchy white to make roughly shaped snowballs. Armed, they each caught the eye of a target. Then, WHOOSH! A five-minute flurry of disintegrating frozen missiles randomly thudding against walls, windows, lampposts, bodies, and heads.

While the crispy chaos continued, Miss Merrick casually constructed an arsenal of the most beautiful rounded snowballs, which she arranged neatly at her feet – a pile of six crisp white weapons of Miss Merrick destruction.

She bent down slowly and picked up a sphere. She raised it and closed her left eye, selecting her target. The snowball cut a line through the crowd like a rocket. Miss Merrick was a champion rounders player at university and still had a throwing arm like a piston.

The sphere found its target … THWACK!

Billy Clarke jumped – his head was jerked sideways by the missile, as it filled his left ear with snow. He looked around in the direction of the throw for someone to growl at.

'Come on now, class. On the bus please.' Miss Merrick was halfway across the road, stopping the traffic for them to cross. She smiled wryly to herself and casually kicked the remaining snowballs as she ushered everyone across to the coach.

The silence was almost deafening when it snowed. Maybe because people couldn't drive their cars and you could hear more than just the drone of engines. If you listened carefully, you could hear the sound of everything – even your own heartbeat.

Charlie was last on the coach.

He stood with Miss Merrick for a moment. The thick crunchy white erased everything that was there before, reflecting the street lights, which made night look like day.

Charlie looked up. Miss Merrick was still for ages, a cloud of breath the only sign she was still alive. He looked where she looked, back to the clean, sparkly white blanket covering the car park. He hadn't noticed there was a bank lined with trees and bushes behind the pool.

A small stream divided the bank, rippling its way over a bed of small, rounded, mustard grey and white stones. The snow had a way of turning the volume down, so the gentle ripple of the stream could be heard.

Tall trees lined the far bank. Bushes lined the nearer one. Covered in heavy snow it looked like every Christmas card Charlie had ever seen. A crow jumped from a branch and flew off. The snow fell from his branch, smashing onto the one below, cascading to a huge cloud of white powder that floated off in the breathy cold.

'Beautiful, isn't it?' Miss Merrick broke the silence.

'Yes, Miss,' Charlie replied.

'I love this time of year, Charlie. There's something magical about it.' She seemed to snap herself back to reality, shaking her head. 'Okay, on the bus, young Sir.

Otherwise we'll be late.' She hopped up the two steps on to the coach.

Charlie picked up his bag and noticed hundreds of tiny footprints. The spider just avoided getting left behind. As he nudged it with his toe a pair of snow-covered eyebrows appeared from the middle of his rolled-up towel.

'C-cold,' the spider whispered in a cloud of breath as he dropped back into the towel. Charlie shook his head and trotted up the steps. The door closed behind him and the driver set off, destroying the new snow with tyre tracks. As he looked back they were already being erased by bigger flakes as the snow got heavier.

Fifteen

Lush Fluffy Dumplings

Snow changed the entire school routine. Parents, or in Charlie's case, Tiffany had to call in each day to make sure the school would be open. Kids disappeared into large padded clothes that they couldn't see out from. As the weather worsened, herds of stiff gingerbread children walked the streets, not able to bend arms or legs or to look around. Not even able to scratch bums or pick noses.

Some parents abandoned their cars. They chose to drag their kids to school on sleds. For most, it was an excuse to show off the expensive pink snow suit and matching boots they'd bought to go on the ski holiday. Other parents were just a little touched in the head and used the snow as an excuse to go sledding after dropping the kids off. They couldn't wait to get into the park opposite the school.

High Hill was the perfect sledding hill. It was a huge steep horseshoe mound which extended up about twenty metres. It was usually crowded with a continuous stream of wheezing runners and shouty aggressive fitness types carrying backpacks full of stones or sand. But nobody was around while the snow fell.

The 'not entirely normal' parents bundled their kids into school with a quick kiss and armfuls of book bag and lunch, then headed to the hill. The competition for the best spot started well before they got there. The casual speed walking looked anything but casual as they walk raced along the pavement and into the park. Being first on the hill was VERY important. Making the first two tracks in that crisp white blanket meant you were a special parent – but the wrong kind of special.

Having fought for the privilege, they pushed off into freedom with legs out and hair flapping in the wind. For a second they were transported back where all the worries of adulthood disappeared and smiles were so tight they hurt. Passers-by could be forgiven for thinking there had been an accident in the park as laughing bodies rolled off their sleds at the bottom of the hill and piled up.

Friday was a non-day at school because of the snow. The hurricane wind whipped up a blizzard as dark clouds poured out tons of the white stuff. School closed early because the head was concerned about becoming snowed in.

The blizzard continued all weekend. Charlie's mum said it was soup weather.

She and Charlie walked to the shops on Saturday afternoon. Mum said she would ask Tiffany to help with her Nan's famous leek and potato soup with HUGE dumplings. Her return from Ireland coincided with a soup day. It's unlikely it actually was famous. Charlie couldn't recall seeing leek and potato soup mentioned on the six o'clock news and it was definitely not in the Big Brother house or part of a bush-tucker trial. But when something's nice, people tend to say it's famous.

'Mum, what's dumplings?' Charlie asked.

Mum looked at him, astonished that he didn't know. 'Dumplings are big warm hugs in freezing cold weather. No matter what's happening, they pick you up and make everything okay again.'

'What's in them?' he asked.

Mum thought for a moment. 'Fat and flour mostly.' She did the guilty face that she did when she was eating chocolate or had one too many glasses of wine and realised she'd polished off the bottle.

'Eeew, yuk!' Charlie screwed up his face in disgust.

'Trust me, they are LUUUSH!' she said in a deep growly voice.

Charlie stopped in his tracks and stared. She used THAT word. The word she used about horse feed cereal that wasn't nice at all. The word she used about dresses and men she liked when she was around her friends. The same word she just used about dumplings.

'They are not LUSH, Mum. Because LUSH isn't a word. They might be nice, but they are not LUSH.'

Charlie conjured up the best professor voice he could find inside his nine-year-old body.

They spent hours making famous Nan soup. Mum showed Charlie how to chop leeks and peel potatoes without including fingers in the dish. She explained what suet was and why throwing flour at her wasn't really a good idea – and they made dumplings. The most enormous fluffiest dumplings anyone had ever seen. Tiffany busied herself around the kitchen, moving and banging things together, until everything was washed up and where it should be again.

They carefully placed the twelve oatmeal coloured billowy clouds in the cauldron – the biggest shiny pot in the kitchen. Sort of round in shape and spongy when poked, the dumplings filled the pot. Charlie was asked not to poke them, but they seemed to call out to him- he couldn't resist.

He and Mum made a deal: that he would keep an open mind about the old-fashioned soup pillows. In exchange they would snuggle with toffee popcorn and chocolate while watching his favourite superhero film.

Mum said this kind of soup called for the BIG bowls.

She kept the BIG bowls at the back of the spinning thing in the corner of the kitchen – the plate, bowl, sandwich toaster, and coffee maker merry-go-round.

Mum took out three deep white bowls big enough to engulf Charlie's head. She gave them a quick wash and dry then placed two on the dining table placemats, either side of the table. Tiff had an important call to make to her boyfriend in Ireland, so decided to eat in her room.

The cauldron took centre stage on a trivet, barely visible through the clouds of volcanic steam pumping through the mass of dumplings on top.

'One or two dumplings, Sir?' she enquired, tea towel draped over one arm like a waiter.

'One please, serving lady.' He chuckled. She dived into the steam through the dumpling mound, scooped up a huge ladle of thick, golden soup and one of the bread things. She did the same for herself then slid a bowl across to Charlie. He stared at the fluffy mound before attacking it with his spoon – prod, cut, blow blow blow, and into his mouth.

Mum watched with interest as he juggled the steamy soup to avoid burning himself. Finally he chewed … and chewed. Eyebrows up. Eyebrows down. Eventually he swallowed and placed his spoon hand on the table.

'Can we have these again, please? They are LUSH!'

Mum laughed. 'I told you. Nothing beats Nan's soup and dumplings when the weather is like this. By the way Sir …'

Charlie looked up.

'I don't believe "lush" is actually a word. I remember someone telling me that.' They laughed and dived back into the soup.

They spent the rest of Saturday watching a marathon of superhero films in a duvet camp, with a huge supply of chocolate and cherryade. Charlie said it was lush and couldn't wait to do it again.

Drunk on soup, popcorn, chocolate, and superhero films, thoughts of Billy Clarke and the dark lord's minions were filed away to the back of his mind – for now.

Sixteen

A Series of Unfortunate Coincidences

Monday rolled around again. Mum called the office and took some time off because of the snow. She was owed time anyway and decided she'd rather not fight the other office types going to the station. It was bad enough ordinarily. She wasn't about to leave a warm and comfy house for a space on the train, under the armpits of soap-dodging smelly people.

Tiffany called the school for the daily snow update.

'*Thank you for calling. The school will be open today, at least initially. Parents should be on high alert, in case an abominable snowball falls on the school, or we run out of supplies. If that happens, all parents will be contacted by text, phone, telepathy, or smoke signals to collect their children. We advise you to collect children as quickly as possible, in case we get snowed in and the dinner ladies get hungry.*

If you know the person you would like to speak to, press one.'

Okay, that wasn't the real message. But it should have been. The real message was boring. The school was open, but would close early because they expected a blizzard.

Mum said Charlie was still on a high from a great weekend, floating around in soup and dumpling hangover. This was much the same as the pizza hangovers he got when he ate a whole pepperoni pizza to himself.

Naaa. Couldn't be, he thought. *There were no gale force farts.* But it could have been an overdose of chocolate.

It was a while before he noticed things missing from around the house. His toothbrush was gone. He couldn't find his lunchbox, and Mum was complaining that her elastic hairbands and baby powder had disappeared.

While brushing his teeth with his finger – which is not easy – Charlie imagined what a toothbrush, lunchbox, baby powder, and hairband thief might look like. He put together his own mental photo-fit. Anyone needing those items must have long hair, bad teeth, sweaty armpits, and a spare sandwich. Hardly the physical make-up of a master criminal. Such a person would be very easy to catch.

Back in his room, he heard strange noises coming from under the bed. He hadn't seen much of Dudley over the weekend. He'd said something about visiting his new friend Aubrey at the swimming pool. Charlie was concerned about his friend making the long journey. But he was a bit of a rugby playing super spider. So, he didn't worry too much.

As he approached the bed, the noises got louder. He swished back the duvet, dropped to his knees, and peered under the bed. The noises stopped instantly. The light was off and Dudley was in the far corner, in shadow. He froze in the way people do when they're caught doing something they shouldn't be. He put four hands behind his back, and Charlie heard something drop to the floor. Dudley swept a back leg around, as though to move something behind him.

'Morning, Dudley, everything okay?' Charlie enquired, not mentioning the suspicious noises.

The spider looked guilty. He edged into the light slowly, stretched three front legs up, and did a huge yawn – trying to be casual, but failing terribly. The rugby boot fell off his artificial foot and hit him on the head.

'All good, Sir. Just had a bad dream and fell out of bed. That might have been the noise you heard.' He smiled a very dodgy smile.

'School's open. Are you coming in?' Charlie asked.

'Sure. Give me a minute to get myself ready.'

They met in the kitchen. Dudley would normally jump onto the counter and wait for Charlie to open the lunchbox. When the coast was clear he'd hop in next to Charlie's favourite packet of Cheesy Puffs, where he pinched one or two when he got peckish. Unusually, he didn't do that today. Today he jumped up onto the counter, milled around for a bit, then hopped down on to Charlie's sleeve and into his coat pocket. He didn't even ask where the lunchbox was. Something wasn't right.

The combination of snow and Christmas meant there wasn't much going on at school. Normal lessons gave way to making Christmas decorations for the classroom. It was the time of year that kids loved. Relaxed and friendly teachers laughed and joked with everyone. They replaced their normal shouty selves with funny and stupid Santa hat wearing people that only appeared at Christmas.

Miss Merrick was 'old school' and a little stingy. She wouldn't buy decorations for the classroom when she worked at a school that had more paper than a paper factory. She had the class cut strips of coloured paper to make paper chains. Every year she did the same thing. She wouldn't spend a penny on 'disgusting' and 'awful' shiny plastic decorations. She much preferred to cover every available space on the doors, walls, and notice boards with her own stuff.

She handed out strips of coloured paper to the girls, who got into groups of five.

'You take the first strip and go round until the two ends touch.' She held a piece of coloured paper and demonstrated, but taped the paper to her sleeve and then taped her fingers together. She shook it off and had another go.

'Then tape them together. The next strip goes through and like this.' She demonstrated the next step. 'Please alternate colours, girls.'

Robert had come back to class with half an eyebrow and a red line with dots and yellow skin around his eye. But he was glad to be back with his friends. He, Charlie, Molly, Bethany, and Nathan were given the job of making paper snowflakes. Miss Merrick gave them folded sheets of paper in various sizes, with lines drawn on. All they had to do was cut where she had drawn and unfold the paper. She demonstrated, turning the paper round with each little detailed cut.

'Then cut here. Here, and here.' Small confetti-sized pieces of paper fell to the floor.

As she turned the paper, holes began to appear. Then she stopped and started to unfold. That was when she realised she'd cut a hole in her Christmas jumper, which now only had one holly berry on top of the Christmas pudding.

She handed out the folded sheets and they began to chop away with coloured plastic scissors, chatting as they worked.

Billy Clarke and his dark minions were in a group on their own. The other classmates gravitated to their own groups, leaving them alone. Miss Merrick gave them snowmen to cut out – folded sheets marked in much the same way as the snowflakes. She didn't demonstrate. Just handed them paper and scissors with instructions to keep to the lines.

Surrounded by the din of snipping and chopping, Miss Merrick wandered around the groups, checking everyone had ten fingers and no holes in their clothes.

By break time she advised the girls to divide their paper chain. The very industrious group had produced a monumental chain, about twenty metres long. The enormous red, pink, yellow, and green snake cascaded off the desk and into coils that spread under the desk and back on itself about fifty times.

The girls had a serious production line going. One supplied paper strips. One tore pieces of tape and lined them up for when they were needed. Another stuck the pieces of paper together and guided the snake under the desk. When they got bored they swapped jobs without missing a beat.

While they worked the snow fell outside. Large wet flakes piled on the snow that had already fallen. The new white blanket meant nobody was allowed out during break. Disappointing in the extreme! Making Christmas decorations was fun. But nowhere near as much fun as whacking someone in the face with a huge wet snowball.

Health and Safety rules meant they had to stay indoors. Health and Safety rules are written by wonderful government people, who love everyone and don't want anyone to die. But obviously these people never had fun, EVER!

They made the rule that a snow-covered playground was far too dangerous. So, children had to be locked in the building making Christmas decorations. Which was acceptable and not child labour at all. Charlie thought they were more likely to die of boredom and wondered if there was a Health and Safety rule for that.

As usual, Billy Clarke and his group couldn't do anything without messing it up. Grandma Joseph decided cutting out snowmen wasn't exciting enough for their group, so he cut out a pair of stupid glasses, held them up to his face and said;

'Eh Clarkie … Clarkie? Who am I?' He mocked in a high cartoon voice. 'Now come on class. Cut out flippin' silly snowmen and bloody stupid snowflakes.'

He stood up and pranced around, making silly noises, pretending to be Miss Merrick. It started them off. The rest continued with decorations, while the minions and the dark lord turned up the volume.

'That's enough, gentlemen. Please sit down. It would be nice to get these decorations done before lunchtime.'

'*Would you please sit down, gentlemen*!' Billy Clarke mocked.

In the chaos, one of the other minions noticed Charlie's red lunchbox on the desk behind the group making snowflakes. He carefully crept across the classroom close to Miss Merrick's desk, where Charlie and friends busied themselves. He quietly took the lunchbox and crept back to the dark lord's group.

'Billy … Billy,' he whispered. 'Look what I've got.' He brought the lunchbox from under the desk. The minions stopped cutting and fencing with the scissors.

Grandma Joseph sarcastically announced the find.

'OH, DEAR! Look what someone left lying around. I wonder who this could belong to. I wonder what's inside?'

Everyone looked across as he began to open the lunchbox. A little crowd of nasties gathered around him as he gazed towards Charlie, smug.

How did it get …? Charlie thought, confused.

'Any spiders in here today, Ginge?' He teased Charlie by opening and closing the box, while the group around him cheered.

Miss Merrick had had enough. She stood up and made her way to the back of the class where the mob had gathered. She took three steps to the row leading around the horseshoe and …

BOOOM!

Everyone jumped up as a huge explosion of white powder blasted out of the lunchbox, into Grandma Joseph's face. Shocked off his feet, he flew backwards over the desk behind, smashing into the chairs and on to the floor.

The white cloud hovered in the air for ages, before settling and revealing the damage it had done. Little by little the picture cleared and everyone could see that Billy Clarke and his minions were covered from head to foot in a mass of white powder. Sitting silent, they looked very much like a group of the snowmen they should have been cutting out.

Almost on cue, the whole class and Miss Merrick erupted in uncontrollable laughter. They couldn't help themselves, it was just so funny. Miss contained herself just enough to say,

'Okay, class, time for lunch. See you back here at half past one. We're putting the decorations up.'

She continued, 'Gentlemen. Wait right there. I'll get you some help.' She filed out behind everyone else, laughing all the way to the head teacher's office.

Dudley watched from the shadows under Miss Merrick's desk. As the classroom emptied he smiled to himself, slinked out towards Charlie's desk, inside the arm of his coat, and back into the pocket – where he stayed for the rest of the day.

Seventeen

The Lunch Box Plan Mystery

The dark lord and his minions didn't have the opportunity to cause as much tension while the snow was around. Kids didn't venture into the playground much because they were incapable of something called common sense. Everything needed to be surrounded with huge red and white plastic pillars and enormous quantities of tape, with words like WARNING or CAUTION. Or big yellow signs with pictures of people flying into the air, which were more funny than scary.

This put teachers in the difficult position of entertaining kids inside. It wasn't difficult at Christmas because the shiny merry this and frosty jingle that were everywhere to keep them occupied.

While teachers were on hand to jump on any hint of bullying, the Christmas spirit flowed through the school. The snow clipped Clarkie's wings and he wasn't happy – but more so because he went home covered in baby powder.

Charlie went home full of the joys of the season. After all, he wasn't covered in baby powder and they were all safe with snow on the ground.

The BBC weather folks had issued ongoing ski, husky, and sled warnings for the weeks leading to Christmas. It looked like it might be a merry Christmas after all with snow on the ground and freedom from the house of Clarkie.

Charlie couldn't contain his euphoria. The kind of happy that makes a nine-year-old grip his own hands as tight as humanly possible, grit his teeth, and rumble shake inside – he couldn't wait to tell Mum about what happened. For a moment he did wonder how his lunchbox had turned up in the classroom as a powder bomb. But he put that out of his mind for the time being; one thing at a time.

Mum surprised him. She wasn't terribly impressed at the happiness over the dark lord and minions getting powder bombed. He sort of forgot that he'd kept her in the dark over what had happened since Clarkie had arrived in September. A little disappointed, he decided to share the moment with his best mate instead, but couldn't find him anywhere. One minute he was tucked up in Charlie's coat pocket. The next he'd pulled a disappearing act.

I know, he thought. He bounded up two stairs at a time and down the hallway, before deliberately slowing and wafting into the bedroom, theatrical style.

'Dudley … DUDLEY! Oh best friend of mine. Where are you?' Charlie called. He dropped to his knees and did a quick three hundred and sixty degree sweep. No sign of the little fuzzy monster.

A more detailed search was required. He scoured the wooden floor on his hands and knees, looking for dark fuzzy contrast against the shiny honey-coloured planks. Under the desk- nope. By the wastepaper basket- nope. Behind the chest of drawers- nope. He wasn't anywhere.

Charlie worked his way around the bedroom from the door to the desk but couldn't find the spider. He decided to give up. Placing his hands on the desk he stood up and could not believe what he saw. Right in front of him, next to the computer and under the desk lamp, was … HIS LUNCHBOX! The one he couldn't find before going to school. The one Grandma Joseph stole and teased him with – the one that had a powder bomb inside.

He rushed over to the bed and swished back the duvet in the hope Dudley was there. Nope! No Dudley, but there was a note on the bed.

Charlie,

Sorry mate. Had to pop out to see a friend. Will be back as soon as possible.

Don't worry, I'm safe. D x

Charlie read it and placed it back on the bed. As he looked back towards the wall he noticed a large, part-rolled sheet of paper with drawings on. It looked like a designer or architect drawing. The kind builders use to build houses.

The rolled sheet had been leaning against Charlie's chest of drawers, but fell down and unrolled – revealing the drawing. Charlie picked it up and unrolled it on the floor in front of the bed, keeping it open with a running shoe at one end and a snow-globe at the other.

It took a couple of seconds for the drawing to register.

Plan 2.01A   *Elastic Driven Powder Bomb*

It seemed to be a detailed engineering plan for the development of a powder bomb, including a shopping list of parts and step by step instructions for assembly.

The component parts:

1. A box with lid

2. One large or two smaller elastic bands

3. A large lolly stick or toothbrush

4. A packet of flour or talcum powder.

Instructions for assembly:

1. *Take elastic band and fasten it to either side of the box widthways, about halfway, either with drawing pins or staples.*
2. *Fill box with powder of your choice.*

3. *Put lolly stick or toothbrush in the centre of the box, between the elastic and twist until very tight. Carefully close box to hold in place. Make sure box is securely closed to prevent accidental firing.*
4. *Place in position and wait for victim to open.*

Stunned, Charlie wondered what he should do with the information. Should he tell Dudley he had found the plan? Or just put it back and say nothing?

A million questions raced through his head. Why hadn't Dudley told him what he'd planned? He quickly rolled up the plan and carefully replaced it where it was. He didn't want the spider to know he'd seen it.

For the time being he'd keep quiet. He was proud that his friend was backing him up, but this seemed a little extreme. He needed time to think. Maybe Dudley was right – perhaps he should tell Mum and the teachers about the hell he and his friends endured from Clarkie. He'd sleep on it and decide later.

The school message lady said the wrong kind of snow fell Monday night and it caused problems with teachers travelling to school and with the heating system. School would be closed.

Charlie wondered what the wrong kind of snow looked like. He'd never seen snow he didn't like. Perhaps the wrong snow was the large grey kind you might find at the beach. The type called stones. Otherwise, was there a wrong kind of snow?

As far as Charlie was concerned, if it was cold, wet, white, fell from the sky and could be slid on, it was the right kind of snow.

He looked out of the window and said to himself, 'Hmmm, what should I do today? No school – apparently there's the right kind of snow in the park and there's a sled in the cupboard under the stairs.' He took less than point two of a second to decide.

'Muuuuum? As there's no school, can I go sledding in the park today?' he called from the bedroom.

'Yeesssss!' she shouted back an extended reply.

The day sorted, he had to find that spider …

Eighteen

The Locked Stockroom

Snow day was a short day. No sooner had Charlie launched himself from High Hill than it became dark and he had to go home.

Dudley was back from his visit to his friend. Frozen, Charlie put the sled back in the cupboard under the stairs and went up to his room to get changed. As he opened the door he could hear humming from under the bed.

He slipped off his snow clothes, jumped into his favourite, slightly wiffy shorts and tee shirt, and jumped on the bed. The humming stopped. Leaning over the side of the bed Charlie balled his hand into knocking knuckles and knocked on the duvet.

'Uh-hum. Knock knock!' He had to make the noise as knocking on a duvet doesn't make much sound.

Dudley's head appeared between the bottom of the duvet and the floor. Nose to nose they smiled broadly. The spider had the sort of twinkle in his eye people get when they're very pleased to see you.

'Can I help you, Sir? You knocked on my duvet.'

Charlie wondered if he should mention the plan he found. He considered it for a few seconds. The question formed in his brain, travelled around his head, down into his throat, edging closer to his mouth. Then his brain quickly sent a CANCEL IMMEDIATELY! notice – the way it does when you're about to say something really stupid.

Charlie smiled a warm smile back instead.

'I missed you today. Glad you're back,' he said. Dudley popped out and on to the bed. The pair spent the evening chatting like the old days, only pausing to make a pile of jam sandwiches and grab Cheesy Puffs and cherryade.

The school message lady informed Mum the school was open Wednesday. It was 'all systems go' at seven o'clock as the military machine kicked into high gear. Breakfast loops splashed with milk – gone in a flash – bowl in the sink. Up to the bathroom – shower? No. A spray of man-in-a-can would be just fine. *I don't smell that much*, Charlie thought, sniffing himself.

Lunch made by Café Mum and on the counter. Clothes flung on and downstairs two at a time. Health and Safety warning about jumping downstairs imparted by Mum;

shoes on. Padded sleeping bag coat on; spider in lunchbox and … let's go!

Mum snowploughed her way to the school.

When they arrived, one of the office ladies tried to catch Charlotte's attention by jumping up and down, waving wildly. The windmill impression did the trick. She crunched along the path to the main doors with Charlie. The door swung open and the office lady guided them to the head teacher's office.

Charlie had never had to go to the head teacher's office. That was a privilege reserved for the naughty kids, or those getting bad news. Nervous, he looked around at the pictures from past and present pupils.

So this is where all the pictures go, he thought. He assumed they were dumped or sold to one of those TV auction programmes to raise money for the school.

The head teacher came in and shook Charlotte's hand.

'Thanks for coming in, Charlotte, if I can call you Charlotte,' Mrs Morris said.

'That's fine,' Mum replied with an edge to her voice, not knowing why they had been called into the office.

Mrs Morris sat on the edge of her desk in front of them.

'Can I ask if there's a problem?' Charlotte enquired.

'Well, it's a rather serious matter,' Mrs Morris replied. 'I don't know if you heard, but on Monday some children in Charlie's class opened a lunchbox which was rigged as a practical joke. Nobody got seriously hurt, but parents are furious they were covered in baby powder and are pressing us to investigate the matter. As the lunchbox was Charlie's we have to ask what he knows about the situation.'

Charlotte reached down to the floor and came up slowly. She held out a fist clutching the handle of Charlie's red lunchbox.

'Do you mean this lunchbox? The lunchbox Charlie has been using for three years? The lunchbox he always brings to school – unless it's dirty and needs a wash, like it did on Monday.

The same lunchbox I put in the dishwasher and forgot to get out. Are you talking about this lunchbox?' She became quite angry and it showed. Growly Mum made an appearance.

People didn't mess with Charlotte. If they did, they soon regretted their mistake. As a solicitor she knew how to work with words. Mrs Morris was on shaky ground and she knew it. She had managed to bring out the solicitor *and* growly Mum. Not a great combination. The situation was unlikely to end well for her. Charlie felt sorry for her, for about ten seconds, then sat proud as he watched his mum go to work on Mrs Morris.

'Oh dear. There seems to have been a mistake. I am ever so sorry. I can't apologise enough.'

Growly solicitor Mum took her first turn.

‘So, let me get the situation clear in my mind. You have accused my son of doing something, before having all the facts to hand. Is that correct?’ She adopted her solicitor tone.

‘Erm, as I said Charlotte. I am sorry.’ Mrs Morris tried to test her with an official tone that might have worked on most people. But not on growly solicitor Mum. She seemed to anger the beast.

‘Let me tell you what’s going to happen, Mrs Morris. The next thing you’re going to do is dictate a sincere letter of apology to myself and Charlie. Because he has been wrongly accused of something he had nothing to do with. The second thing you’re going to do is overlook any absence during term time if I feel that Charlie needs a holiday to recover from being wrongly accused. Is that acceptable? Or should I draft a letter to the Board of Governors with details of the incident?’

Mrs Morris opened her mouth to agree just as Molly ran in, out of breath.

‘Miss! Miss! Miss Merrick asked me to get you. James Backworthy went to get some books from the stockroom and is locked in. The caretaker needs permission to break the door down.’

Another of Clarkie’s minions, James Backworthy usually added a bit more nasty when Clarkie finished his bullying. A true git, he laughed in Molly’s face and knocked a packet of crisps on her when Clarkie pushed her off the lunch benches and she lay on the floor.

Charlotte looked at Mrs Morris, who was clearly getting in a flap.

'I'm sorry – you can see I have to go. Charlie, make your way to class and please don't mention this conversation to anyone. Thank you. I'll send that letter as soon as possible.' She rushed out and down the corridor towards the stockroom, where Miss Merrick and the caretaker tried to calm Mr Backworthy, who could be heard inside, crying and banging on the door.

Charlie kissed Mum on the cheek and made his way down the corridor to class. He stopped outside, placed the lunchbox on a stack of lunch room chairs, wrestled his coat off, then popped the lid of the box to check on his pal.

The spider had gone AWOL again.

Nineteen

The Panic Room

That Wednesday Miss Merrick wanted to ramp up the Christmasivity in class and so decided to do a play with the kids.

The classroom already looked incredible, covered in hand-made Christmas tat. Multi-coloured chain snakes slithered around the walls and onto the ceiling, meeting at the light in the centre of the room. Questionable snow-ish flakes adorned the walls and noticeboards. Dozens of red-nosed reindeer pulled sleighs. Bright red Santas and huge snowmen covered ever other available space.

Miss Merrick went to great expense to make her corner as Christmassy as possible. She had holly and berries, Christmas puddings, reindeer, Santas, and a large Nativity scene next to her desk. She even bought twinkly lights and large sheets of white fleece, which she attached to the wall behind her with a power stapler. She created a grotto in the corner and loved sitting there, like a tiny vampire elf.

Miss Merrick liked to go the extra mile if she committed to a project, as the caretaker had discovered on snow day Tuesday.

While doing his odd jobs in school, he heard a frequent thump and echo coming from Miss Merrick's classroom. As it was a snow day, nobody was supposed to be at school, so he walked down to investigate.

It was impossible to see past the Christmas tat plastered all over the door and windows. So he twisted the wobbly handle and swung the door open. Miss Merrick stood on a chair behind the desk with a huge piece of fleece in one hand and a massive red power stapler in the other. She removed it from the large leather tool belt around her waist, where screwdrivers and hammers clinked together.

'*Oh, the weather outside is frightful* … BANG!' She sang Christmas songs as she stapled. '*And the fire is so delightful* … BANG!'

She didn't hear him come into the classroom, so he quietly backed out and closed the door. She seemed to have the situation under control.

Miss Merrick had chosen an alternative to the traditional Christmas play. They would be working on *Frankenstein and the Mummy Save Santa* for a few lessons leading up to the big Christmas assembly. The plan was to perform in front of the school if they could refine it.

She asked James Backworthy to get the books from the English stockroom next to the boy's toilet. It was never locked. There was no real need to as nobody really wanted to mess with heaps of old dusty books.

James Backworthy was a small, harsh-looking weasel child with pointed features – even his teeth looked pointed. He looked unwashed and smelly. The kind of child that might have been called "flea-bag" by children or some other equally nasty name. His shirt collar looked crumpled up and pushed into the neck of his sweater which was half tucked into trousers. The look was topped off with one sleeve rolled and the other dangling loose.

Nobody knew why he had such a chip on his shoulder. Perhaps being one of the smallest people at school annoyed him. Maybe he felt inadequate because everyone else seemed smarter. Nobody knew why he acted like a git; but he did.

Mr Backworthy had teamed up with Clarkie when he arrived, but he was horrible before – the kind of child who wasn't smart enough to be ignorant and probably couldn't spell it. Generally a nasty piece of work, he enjoyed the misfortune of others and added to it if he could.

As expected, Mr Backworthy protested because Miss Merrick had the audacity to ask him to do something. He whined sitting at his desk. He complained standing up. He whinged while walking to the door, and moaned walking along the corridor to the stockroom. He complained the entire time.

While he was getting the books Miss Merrick started to give people their parts in the play. She pulled a copy of the book from the grotto behind her desk. They were ten minutes in when the classroom door crashed open, knocking down two Santas and a snowman.

James Backworthy couldn't get out of the stockroom. The teacher next door had rushed to help when she heard him crying and pounding on the door. She tried to open the door but it was locked and full of glue.

'That's impossible,' Miss Merrick said. 'That stockroom hasn't been locked in years. Nobody even knows where the key is.'

'That may be the case, Miss. But he is definitely locked in there. I tried to let him out myself.'

They hurried out of class and down the corridor to the stockroom. Miss Merrick sent Molly to get Mrs Morris, the head teacher.

Miss Merrick, the head teacher, and the caretaker met at the stockroom. The caretaker pushed and jiggled the door, confirming suspicion that it was locked and had a quantity of glue inside the keyhole to prevent it from being unlocked.

'The only way to get in is to break the door open,' he said.

Mr Backworthy could be heard banging and shouting.

'HELLLLLP! HELLLLLP! GET ME OUT! IS SOMEONE COMING? I NEED THE TOILET!'

Mrs Morris gave the caretaker permission to break the door open. Everyone stood back as he readied himself to bash it with his shoulder.

'Stand well back from the door, fella!' he shouted through the door to Mr Backworthy. Then he stepped back, gritted his teeth, and rammed the door with his shoulder.

BOOM! It didn't budge. He rocked back again and BOOM! Nothing. One more try – BOOM! The door creaked slightly, but didn't open.

He rubbed his shoulder and looked towards Mrs Morris.

'We're going to need something a little more serious. Is that okay?' he said.

'What's more serious?' she replied.

'I think a small sledgehammer should do it. One tap and that'll open right up.' He sounded more confident.

'Okay,' Mrs Morris agreed. 'But please be quick. There's a scared young man in there.'

The caretaker had a small room at the front of the school. He went off and was back in a couple of minutes, carrying what looked like a chunk of steel on a long blue stick. He cleared everyone around the door, approached, and placed the hammer head against the handle. He drew the head back, took a swing, and …

BOOM!

CRUNCH! RATTLE! PING!

The door flew open, whacking the wall behind. A huge piece of plaster flew off and smashed into the bookshelves. The lock disintegrated as the hammer struck. Pieces flew off everywhere, leaving a shiny swinging mess where the handle used to be.

As they looked into the room, James Backworthy stood crying with a pile of books at his feet. As the dust cleared everyone saw the huge dark patch at the front his trousers.

Twenty

Silly Billy Swim Trunks

The Thursday of snow week was the class swimming lesson. Charlie had to rescue plastic bricks again. You would have thought the swimming teachers would be more careful with their plastic bricks, once they were retrieved – but no. In a typically careless fashion, they dropped them in the pool again.

Miss Merrick finally got the copies of *Frankenstein the Mummy Save Santa* she needed. Luckily, James Backworthy didn't get any of them wet during the unfortunate incident, so she had just enough copies for the whole class. They greeted the play with confusion, grunts, sighs, and moans. How could Frankenstein and the Mummy possibly save Santa? Miss Merrick explained, at considerable speed. She cleared her throat and went for it.

'*Frankenstein and the Mummy Save Santa* is the story of Jake Rust who has a Christmas wish granted by the Weihnachtengeist pretending to be Santa Claus. The Weihnachtengeist is the Anti-Christmas ghost that wants to take over and wreck Christmas. The Geist can take various forms to trick people into making a wish. If they do, the wish is granted, but this allows the Geist and his evil helpers into the real world. They can then wreak havoc on Christmas. In this story, Jake wishes that everything in his imagination is brought to life. The Geist grants his wish then slips into the real world to kidnap Santa. This obviously puts Christmas at risk. Jake then imagines Frankenstein and the Mummy into the real world to help him rescue Santa and save Christmas. Is everyone clear now?'

The class sat stunned with their mouths open. Partly because the story was so ridiculous and partly because the explanation was delivered in a rapid-fire machine-gun style like a rapper, by a teacher who looked like the presenter for an antiques programme.

Miss Merrick could have been a rapper. She was a performance 'slam' poet at university, before performance poetry became mainstream. She was 'spittin' rhymes' in a street style before any of them knew what rhymes were. She would no doubt be the coolest old vampire in the care home when her time came.

She handed out books and gave everyone a character, which they had to learn by lunchtime.

It did not go the way she hoped it might. There were missed out lines; characters confused; some forgot they were even in the play. At one point Bethany played the part of Miss Merrick, who wasn't even in the book.

Billy Clarke strongly objected to being cast as the horrible old Christmas Geist. Moaning was expected from him. That's all he did at school. Moan in class – bully everywhere else.

While he complained, Robert, cast as Frankenstein, walked across the classroom with stiff legs and arms out, groaning in a black and white monster style. Busy moaning, Clarkie didn't notice the Frankenrobert behind him. It reached out and slipped stiff fingers around his neck. He spun round with a glare that could burn holes, but that changed quickly as the Frankenrobert lifted him off his chair by the throat and shook him around.

It took a while for Miss Merrick to realise Clarkie wasn't getting into character, as he wheezed and turned blue. With a little more urgency than usual, she wafted across to peel the Frankenrobert off.

Robert, back to himself, assured her he was in character the whole time. She gave him a knowing look and whispered, 'You seemed to be enjoying your character a little too much. Although I don't blame you – he's a very good character.' She walked away, chuckling.

As usual, the class met at the front gates for the swimming coach. The class normally waited quietly, like nice little people, until Miss Merrick came out. Not today! That went out of the window – because the snow just had to be made into snowballs and they just had to be thrown in the face of your best friend.

Snow fuelled chaos ensued. The boys pelted each other with an arsenal of snowballs. The girls built the most amazing snow models and Bethany was Bethany. She lay on the floor, flicking snow everywhere with her mad arms and legs.

The class boarded the coach and arrived at the pool ten minutes earlier than usual. There wasn't a single vehicle on the road because of wrong snow. Miss Merrick wafted through the doors and everyone raced to the changing rooms for the best spot.

Dudley demonstrated a new move as Charlie flicked him from the centre of his rolled-up towel. He'd been practising. Nobody does three spins, a roll, a flip, then one of those gymnastic finishes, without practising. He said he hadn't, but Charlie wasn't daft.

He went off to swim his two hundred metres certificate and save a lot of bricks. While he did that, Bethany got Molly to watch her dive to the bottom, where she tried to make more snow angels. She didn't grasp that the flapping around looked like drowning when there wasn't any snow.

Billy Clarke clung to the side rail and spent the whole lesson complaining about being splashed, as usual. Dudley disappeared to see his friend Aubrey and Miss Merrick set up camp at the café.

She ordered a huge mug of frothy hot chocolate and an individual pack of custard creams, while she waited for the cast of her play to finish splashing around. She loved hot chocolate, especially when she dropped a pile of small white marshmallows into the cup from the packet she carried in her bag. Marshmallows made an ordinary cup of chocolate just perfect.

The poolside buzzer went off at half past two. No more bricks could be saved. Twenty dripping children emerged from the pool, shivering as they shuffled along the bobbled tiles to their respective changing rooms. Miss checked the time and dunked the second custard cream, just getting it to her mouth before the soggy end fell off.

She met the children at the meeting point, did a swift head count, and made for the doors like Mother Goose with her goslings.

'Miss?' enquired Bethany.

'Yes, Bethany. What can I do for you?' she replied.

'Where's Billy Clarke?' asked Bethany.

Miss Merrick did another head count and clapped her hand to her face as she realised her mistake.

'Oh, dear. I miscounted!' She looked around and settled on Charlie. 'Charlie, would you pop into the changing room to see what happened to Clarkie. Thank you.'

Begrudgingly Charlie made his way back through the swing doors to the boys' changing rooms. Billy Clarke sat on the long slatted bench, under the peg where he'd hung his bag, elbows on his knees and head in hands. Swimming shorts still dripping, there was no sign of a bag, clothes, or his towel.

Charlie approached with caution. It could be a trap – the kind of thing Clarkie would do. Trick someone into coming back to the changing room and push them in the footbath. He stood a safe distance from the git.

'Miss Merrick wants to know why you're taking so long. The coach will be leaving soon.'

Charlie waited; Clarkie didn't answer. He just sat in silence, dripping. Charlie returned to Miss Merrick. 'Miss, I think you should come to the changing room. Clarkie is just sitting there in his swimming shorts. He isn't getting changed.'

Miss Merrick huffed, took her bag off, and asked a member of the pool staff to stand with the children. She wafted through the doors to the changing room, getting more impatient with each step.

'Clarkie. Would you please get dressed – the coach is about the leave. The driver has another job to do and we're making him late. He is not best pleased.'

A voice emerged from the mass of dangling blond hair. 'Can't get changed,' it snapped.

'Don't be silly. What do you mean you can't get changed? That's ridiculous.' Miss Merrick became annoyed.

'ARE YOU DEAF?' Blond hair flicked cold water at her as he turned to shout. 'I CAN'T GET CHANGED! SOMEBODY KNICKED MY CLOTHES!'

It took a while for the statement to sink in.

Confused, she walked around, randomly looking for the missing clothes. She walked along the line of cubicles, flapping doors open in turn, checking behind each one and under the small slatted bench seats.

'Don't bother. I've already checked,' Clarkie conceded.

'Well, Clarkie. Clothes don't just disappear. We have a real problem here,' she said, becoming more panicked by the second.

Back outside, she found the building manager. Charlie could see the conversation through the glass doors. The kind of urgent conversation you don't need to hear – five minutes of pacing up and down doing windmill arms.

The pair eventually went back to the changing room, returning five minutes later – without Billy Clarke. The manager sent search parties through the building, but the clothes could not be found. They'd vanished. Bag, clothes, shoes, and towel – all gone. Billy Clark sat in the changing room with no possessions whatsoever.

At half past three, the coach driver looked at his watch and decided he had to leave. He explained that he sympathised with the problem, but didn't have a choice. It was an impossible position. They would have to sort something or stay at the pool.

Miss Merrick asked the pool manager to look in the lost property box. Sometimes people forgot clothes. It wouldn't be an ideal situation, but lost property clothes would keep Clarkie warm for the journey back to school in the snow. He scoured the building for spares while she got the children on the coach and explained why they were so late.

The driver looked at Miss Merrick, making disappointed faces, tapping his watch continually.

Five minutes later, the pool doors swished open and the manager came out. He walked to the coach with a dark coat-covered bump. Nobody could work out what it was until the doors opened and he removed the coat.

BILLY CLARKE!

He was dressed only in swimming shorts with a red

check tea towel across his shoulders; the only thing the manager could find in the whole building. No shoes or socks. No clothes at all. No bag or towel. Not a stitch.

This was a different Clarkie to the one they were used to. The brash, aggressive, nasty dark lord of the playground was gone, replaced by a more timid and unsure little boy. He shivered, alone in a double seat halfway down the coach. Miss Merrick offered him her cardigan. He snapped a refusal at her.

An uncertain silence filled the bus for a few minutes as they turned out of the car park and on to the road back to school.

Robert spoke first.

'Clarkie? How did you lose your clothes, mate?' Clarkie returned a hateful dark lord stare.

'I didn't LOSE my clothes, you idiot. Someone KNICKED my clothes – IDIOT!'

'Okay, mate. Calm down. Don't be a silly Billy.' Robert giggled to himself and repeated the joke. 'Don't be a silly Billy – that's funny.'

It spread. A ripple of whispers at first: '*Hehe, don't be a silly Billy*,' up and down the aisle. '*Don't be a silly Billy*,' louder and louder until it poured out of every child on the coach.

'He's silly … a silly Billy! Silly Billy! Silly Billy! Silly Billy! Silly Billy!'

A voice shouted, ‘In swim trunks!’ They turned up the volume and looked directly at Clarkie. The worst bully the school had ever known.

‘Silly Billy … Swim Trunks! Silly Billy … Swim Trunks! Silly Billy … Swim Trunks! Silly Billy … Swim Trunks! Silly Billy … Swim Trunks! Silly Billy … Swim Trunks! Silly Billy … Swim Trunks! Silly Billy … Swim Trunks!’

Clarkie’s power was disappearing by the second and he knew it.His parents tried to complain about the incident in the run-up to Christmas. They said they would sue the school for negligence and something called pain and suffering.

His parents tried to complain about the incident in the run-up to Christmas. They said they would sue the school for negligence and something called pain and suffering.

Mrs Morris would have been concerned if each child bullied by Clarkie hadn't told their parents about his reign of terror. They swamped the school with hundreds of letters which she passed to Board of Governors. She was instructed to inform Mr and Mrs Clarke that their son was no longer welcome at Chilverhave Primary.

A new anti-bullying policy was written and a plan made to send teachers on courses to notice the signs of bullying. Children were encouraged to be honest about anything worrying them, to make sure someone like Billy Clarke could never terrorise the school again.

Clarkie did not return after the swim trunks incident. Nobody knew what happened to him. Months later Charlie heard a rumour that his family had moved away. But nobody knew for sure; and they didn't care.

The Christmas preparations continued in Clarkie's absence. Class 5M abandoned their plans to perform *Frankenstein and the Mummy Save Santa*.

The decision followed an unfortunate accident with some loose mummy bandages, a life-size sleigh, and Frankenstein's bolt.

Miss Merrick did the more sensible thing: she found some nice carols and they sang beautifully.

It seemed the Christmas Geist didn't get his way after all.

Christmas was saved.

Twenty and a half

What's This?

It was the week before Christmas.

Charlie arrived home from a Christmas shopping trip with Mum and a certain spider. They dropped the bags, kicked snow off their boots, and put them in the under-stair cupboard. Massive padded coats were placed back on their hooks like a row of floating bodies – and they were home in the warm again.

Mum headed straight to the kitchen, filled the kettle, and flicked the switch. She grabbed a huge mug from the tree on the counter and called Charlie.

'Sweetie? Do you want a cup of tea?' Her words chased him along the hallway and halfway up the stairs. He shouted back as he bounded the stairs two at a time.

'No thanks, Mum. I've still got a small bottle of cherryade in my bag.'

'Okay. By the way – what have I told you about running upstairs two at a time?' She smiled to herself.

Charlie skated into his room in socked feet with a bag full of presents. He planned to wrap them badly and put them under the small tree on his desk. On Christmas Eve they would go under the family tree in the living room.

He changed into his wiffy house clothes and flung himself on the bed and leaned over.

'Knock! Knock! Anyone home?' He knocked on the duvet in the usual way and waited.

'Dudley, you in there?' he called, but didn't get a reply.

'Where is that spider? We just came home together.' He leaned over upside down and swished back the duvet. Dudley wasn't home.

He noticed the plan for the powder bomb was still in the corner, rolled up and ready to be used again, if needed. Dudley could have been one of those hoarders on TV. He had heaps of rubbish. A bit like the Americans on telly, who have to move out of their houses because they have stuff and no space to live.

Charlie looked around.

Dudley had batteries for things he didn't even own. In the far corner, pens and pencils spilled from a case – which explained why Charlie never had any. Next to the case pieces of jigsaw were piled neatly, even though there wasn't actually a jigsaw. A long door key poked out from under the chest of drawers and to the left he saw a tube of superglue and a purple Ysas watch.

The pieces fell into place. Billy Clarke owned a purple designer watch and James Backworthy had been glued in the English stockroom. Clearly a spider had saved Christmas.

Charlie didn't wonder if he should talk to Dudley this time. He replaced the duvet, bounced off the bed, and shouted down to Mum.

'Muuuuuuum. Have you seen Dudley, my spider with an artificial leg?'

Lightning Source UK Ltd.
Milton Keynes UK
UKHW04f0732190918
329148UK00001B/88/P

9 781787 195462